Our Scrappy Queen

THE MEN OF PSYSPECOPS

BOOK 3

KAMERON CLAIRE

SNUGGLE WHORE PRESS, LLC

PSYSPECOPS

OUR
SCRAPPY
Queen
Kameron Claire
USA TODAY BESTSELLING AUTHOR

Dedication

To all the Witty, Wicked & Wild Readers...
Never let them silence our Witty Tongues,
Never let them shame our Wicked Needs,
Never let them stop our Wild Deeds.
If it harm none, do what thy will!

Orgasm Control / Edging Kink

BDSM terminology is vast, varied, and often up to interpretation. For the purpose of this book, these definitions apply to our submissive and her Dominants...

Orgasm control or edging is experiencing the feeling of power that come from controlling their partner's orgasm as form of domination and consensual torture.

There are multiple techniques to control orgasms, but regardless, all techniques should result in amplified orgasm and feelings of euphoria once release is achieved.

ENTES TUERE
PUNIRE IMPIOS

Chapter One

O'DELL

"HEY, O'DELL. SHE'S BACK."

I jump off the couch and run over to the monitors that Dem has had his eyes glued to for the last two hours. "Fuck. What are we going to do about her?"

"I know what I'd like to do with her," Kerr rumbles from the armchair.

"I said *about*—dickhead—not with."

He flips me off but otherwise makes no effort to change his feet up, head back position. "What's she doing?"

"Up to the same old shenanigans. Slinking around the house, looking into windows, leaving love notes on the door. Did Soren find anything on her?"

"No, but to be honest, I didn't ask him to look hard. I really didn't think she'd keep coming back, and the pictures we sent him weren't much to work with."

"I think it's time for one of us to follow her back to her car and at least grab a license plate or something."

That snags Kerr's attention as he sits up. "I volunteer for something."

"Keep it in your pants," I chuckle. "But yeah, get ready to follow her and grab her license plate."

Kerr is lacing up his boots when Dem says, "What the fuck is she doing?"

He maneuvers the cameras and zooms in on the propane tanks feeding the twenty-by-eighty trailer. The guy we've been monitoring for the last three months, Bobby Lash, has been using this piece-of-shit mobile home as a backwoods office and showroom to meet prospective clients looking for girls of varying ages and ethnicities.

He's a human trafficker—a piece of garbage that I'd sooner shoot than deal with—but Bobby is nothing more than a stepping stone to the guy doing the wheeling and dealing for this despicable enterprise: Joey DiFallo, son of Vincent DiFallo, patriarch of one of the oldest organized crime families in Chicago.

That's why we've been sitting out here in the middle of nowhere for three months, waiting for the opportunity to catch him—aka the Big Fish.

This assignment has been by far the most frustrating assignment we've ever worked on. Knowing what he's doing in that trailer, knowing there are women—even worse, girls—being moved in and out of there consistently and not being able to move on them has rubbed me and my partners raw. Sitting by and doing nothing goes against our very nature, but we're trying to keep our eyes on the prize.

At least that's what Townsend, our employer, keeps reminding us.

I pull out our binoculars and go to another window to get a different vantage point of our femme fatale, who has been casing the property and haunting our dreams. Every time she comes here, she's wearing skin-tight black, and every thick curve she has begs to be dominated and controlled. She's the sexiest thing we've seen in a long time and that's not just three months' worth of isolation talking.

I set my sights on her, realizing about the same time Dem does that something is very wrong.

"Fuck. Are those explosives?"

"I think so," Dem calls from his perch in front of the monitor.

"Fuck!" I turn and grab a rifle, pulling my comm piece out of my pocket and sticking it into my ear. We cannot have her blow this place up. Doing so will fuck our entire operation.

Kerr is already on his feet, his go bag on his shoulder, an M4 at his side. He nods his head and taps his ear. "Let's go."

We're held up in a house that overlooks the trailer by a couple of acres. It takes under a minute to run down the hill and crouch behind the trees.

"What's she doing?" Kerr hisses as she runs back to the propane tanks from the trailer's rear door that she's pried open.

I shake my head, signaling to him to take the front of the house while I sneak around the back. I figure we'll surprise her and she'll cower when faced with two large, highly trained men, promising to never come back without asking us questions.

I get to the propane tanks, finding the pressure valve tampered with and a series of fireworks duct taped to the top. Considering she's in the house right now, I'm betting all the burners are wide open. "Shit, man. She's definitely planning on blowing up the house."

"No shit?"

Our gazes connect the moment she exits the property, her blue eyes immediately going to the rifle across my chest. She dashes back into the house, slamming the door shut behind her.

"She's coming your way... watch the front door," I say into my comm.

"Roger that," Kerr responds.

I eye the door, checking the seams with a wary gaze. "Please don't be booby-trapped."

Turning the handle, I slowly open the door, leading with the nozzle of my gun. I don't relish the idea of shooting a woman, but I learned a long time ago never to underestimate an adversary. The smell of gas permeates the air, so my first stop is the stove where I turn off the burners.

Yeah, she's definitely planning to blow this place up, which means we need to get out of here—fast.

"Come on out. You got nowhere to go. My partners are waiting for you outside."

This is my first time inside this shit hole. The living room is passable, the kitchen bare bones, but the primary bedroom with its king-sized bed is immaculate—a real party room—which turns my stomach sour.

Fucking pieces of shit. I can't wait until the day we get to kill these motherfuckers.

I'm moving down the hallway toward the second bedroom when a closet door flings out, knocking me backward. Our intruder jackrabbits out of her hiding space and runs out the back door.

"She's on the move. Back door."

"Left or right?" Kerr growls.

"Fuck if I know."

"Dammit! She's heading south to the road."

I jump out of the back door and run south after Kerr and our mystery intruder. I've got to say, I'm both annoyed and impressed she took me down, even momentarily. He's only a few feet behind her when he jumps and tackles her, taking her to the ground.

But she's spry, rolling out from underneath him and jumping to her feet. Unfortunately for her, Kerr is just as agile and he's on his feet, ready to lunge again. She jumps and spins to perform some kind of roundhouse kick—which looks great in the movies, but isn't really practical in close combat. Kerr grabs her thigh and uses her momentum to throw her to the ground.

At this point, I've slowed to a light jog to enjoy the show. Fighting in the open near the house is not ideal. We need to get out of here before someone drives up, but she's too much fun. The things coming out of her mouth would make the most hardened combat soldiers blush, and she's calling Kerr everything in and out of the book.

"Get off me, you shit-licking piece of soulless garbage!" she screams as he flips her over, putting her face in the dirt. "Fucking prick!"

Kerr looks up at me with a gleam in his eye that is not appropriate given the situation. "You want to fucking help a brother out?"

I grin. "I want to watch her kick your ass some more."

He narrows his eyes. "Bag, twenty yards back."

"Oh," I didn't even notice he shed his bag and gun when he took her to the ground. That would have hurt both of them to tackle her with an M4 across his chest. Not that we haven't done it before in the last thirteen years together.

Kerr, Dem, and I are former PsySpecOps operators. We were teamed by the US Army back when we were eighteen and a few weeks into PsyOps school. PsySpecOps doesn't take volunteers. They recruit the best of the best out of the special forces' units. We were chosen not only for our physical prowess—marksmen, hand-to-hand, endurance, strength, intelligence, instinct, and ingenuity—but also for our psych profiles, which say we'll work best as a team. We're the Army's answer to a super soldier without chemical injections and gamma rays. Together, the three of us are the perfect soldier, accentuating each other's strengths and eliminating any weaknesses.

Needless to say, we get along really well and do everything together. And I do mean everything.

I jog over to his bag, pulling out the Velcro cuffs from the side pocket before flinging the bag over my shoulder.

I also grab his gun, tsking at the mud caked in the muzzle.

She's still fighting him, bucking her ass under his hips —which I know turns him on. It would definitely turn me on.

I throw the cuffs on her back and then bend down so I'm face to face with her. "Do you think grinding your ass into his cock is the brightest idea right now, Cupcake?"

KABOOM!

I'm thrown a good six feet—landing on the two M4s strapped across my chest—as a section of the house explodes. I take a few seconds, or is it minutes, to shake the fog from my brain and assess the situation. Kerr's up on one knee, attempting to find the strength to chase after the woman who just blew up our entire operation.

Lucky for her, our bodies protected her from the blast.

Lucky for all of us, she's quick and took us far enough from the house that we'll walk away from this relatively unscathed—despite a series of cuts and contusions.

I stumble to my feet, my chest screaming with newly forming bruises, and snatch the cuffs off the ground. Chasing after Kerr, who once again is leaping and tack-ling her to the ground, I run up on them at the same time she lands a left hook across his cheek.

"Bitch!" Kerr growls, gripping a handful of her hair and yanking her to her feet. She kicks back, narrowly missing his shin, and that's when I get pissed. I kick the back of her knee, causing her legs to crumble underneath her, all the while Kerr keeps a firm grip on her hair. He shoves her face first into the dirt again, this time with his knee between her shoulder blades to pin her in place. I grab her wrist, securing one and then the other, and then Kerr yanks her up on her feet.

She continues to curse. "Fuck you, you fucking pieces of shit! Now, you'll have to use one of your other kiddie porn, sex-trafficking shit holes to tug each other's microscopic dicks!" She kicks back again at the same time as Dem's voice is in our ears.

"EMS is en route. Get the fuck out of there unless you want to blow our entire cover."

I turn my glare on her. "Listen up, Cupcake. You have two choices. Either you shut up and run with us like a good little captive, or we're going to bind your legs, gag you, and drag you through this fucking forest by your ankles."

"Fuck you!" she screams as loud as possible.

"That's it," I pull a rag out of my back pocket and use my thumb and fingers to pry her mouth open, shoving it in while Kerr holds her in place. Securing it with Coban wrap, I grin as Kerr throws a shoulder into her solar plexus, knocking the wind out of her and giving me precious seconds to secure her ankles before she flails and hurts one or all of us.

"Why does everyone opt to do it the fucking hard way?" I grumble as Kerr hoists her on his shoulder, carrying her out of the field in a fireman's hold.

As soon as we hit the trees, I look back at the house that is engulfed in flames. High-pitched squeals sound off as fireworks ignite—minor explosions and bright colors sparking from behind the blazing inferno.

Kerr chuckles beside me. "A good fight and a show. It must be our lucky day."

I side-eye him, because this is anything but lucky. Three months' worth of surveillance—fucked. What does this mean for the investigation or our involvement? Not a fucking clue.

All I know is Townsend is going to be pissed, and if this spooks the DiFallo family into changing everything about their operation, this chick just painted a huge target on me and my partners. We aren't the only ones who have been stuck on babysitting duty for the last few months, although we are the only ones without a woman waiting for us back home—a sticking point Reese and Lee, my counterparts as team leads, have made multiple times when we've reported into our weekly debriefs. They and their partners—like all ex-PsySpecOps teams— share their lives and their woman.

And the lucky bastards found women who would marry their dumbasses.

I can't even imagine.

Well, that's not true. I can imagine, as I often do when fantasizing about the day that Kerr, Dem, and I find a perfect woman of our own to complete our family.

I glance at the woman tossed over Kerr's shoulder and wonder—have we found her?

ENTES TUERE
PUNIRE IMPIOS

Chapter Two

KERR

I LOVE nothing more than a sexy woman who likes to tumble around on a mat before we tumble around in the sheets, but this chick has pissed me off. My cheek throbs as blood rushes through my veins, exertion causing me to breathe heavily.

"We should get her vehicle off the road before EMS takes note of it," I throw out as a good idea.

O'Dell purposefully makes eye contact with her. "Especially if we have to kill her."

We're not going to kill her, but the threat is out there and has the intended effect if the way she stops squirming is any indication.

I guess he's pissed, too.

The three of us—Dem, O'Dell, and I—are natural predators. We love nothing more than dominating a woman, but this little exchange went from cute to dangerous quickly. I guess there's the whole *she's not our submissive and wants to kill us* thing to bring the mood down, too.

Damn, it's been too long since I've gotten laid and ever since the first time this hellcat popped up on our video surveillance, I've been fantasizing about her.

"I don't suppose you'd tell us where your vehicle is parked so we can avoid your license plate being run in conjunction with a house spontaneously blowing up?" he states behind me.

She's still as the dead for several seconds and then tries to speak through the gag. I halt my forward progression, taking a short breather as I set her on the ground. We're well hidden in the trees, halfway to our safe house on the hill, so O'Dell removes her gag.

"Silver Nissan Sentra parked up from the house, not down. I drove in the back way off Wheeler Road."

"Smart. EMS won't drive past it."

"Neither will your piece of shit boss Bobby," she hisses.

"Boss?" I exchange a glance with O'Dell. She thinks we're employed by that scumbag, which means she thinks we're traffickers, too. She has no idea what kind of shit storm she's stumbled into, but at least we know she's not on their payroll.

Honestly, until this moment, I thought they had sent her to torch any evidence and maybe our three months of surveillance were in vain. I mean, with a destroyed house, they are in vain. I don't begrudge O'Dell having to call this in later, if Dem hasn't already done so.

"Let's get her secured at the house and then we can pick up her car."

I make a move toward her and she kicks her bound legs out at me. "Don't fucking touch me!"

O'Dell is having none of it. Wrapping his hand around her throat, he pins her to the ground. "You have officially entered *fuck around and find out* territory, Cupcake." Then he shoves the rag back into her mouth and pulls the Coban wrap back in place.

"You need a break?" he asks me.

"No, I got her," I hoist her up on my shoulder and smack her ass hard for good measure before completing the climb up the hill. We dump her in the first bedroom, a small one with a twin-sized bed. She bounces unceremoniously on the mattress and, without a backward glance, we shut and lock the door behind us.

"Unfuckingbelievable," O'Dell growls, throwing my go bag on the couch. He hands me my filthy weapon—the one I had just finished cleaning a couple of hours ago.

Dem chirps from the monitors. "Welcome home, boys. By the way, that was entertaining as fuck to watch. Right up to the explosion."

"Yeah. Is EMS onsite yet?" I ask.

"Pulling in now."

"We've got to get down there and remove the cameras before forensics or anyone else notices them," O'Dell grabs two bottles of water, throwing one in my direction.

Dem nods. "We're less than an hour before sunset and it'll take them at least that long to put out the flames and get the scene contained. We'll go after they pull out tonight, but before the morning crew arrives."

"Townsend is going to kill us," O'Dell grumbles, downing his bottle of water before tossing it in the recycling box.

While they are bantering—planning our next series of actions before we head back to Townsend Agency with our tails tucked between our legs—I'm thinking about the hellcat in the next room. She can fight, that's for sure. Tall and sexy, with voluptuous curves and a mouth to make the church moms weep and guys like me hard.

"Who do you think she is?"

O'Dell shakes his head. "Someone that hates Bobby as much as we do."

"Let's go get her car so we can start this interrogation."

"Yeah."

SHE'S smart and I have to wonder if she's had training. Her car is approximately a half-mile from the house, parked on the side of the road in a makeshift parking lot—as if she was a random hiker who parked along the side of the road outside of the state park to avoid fees—something a professional like us would do if we couldn't camouflage our location.

She gave up her keys readily to O'Dell and after

retrieving the vehicle without incident, we're now parked in front of the house. I'm rifling through her center console and glove box while he goes through her bag that was stashed in the backseat.

There's too much information in her car to lead us to believe she is a professional, but she's definitely clever.

"Kyra Stewart, age twenty-eight," O'Dell reads from her license. "Her birthday was two weeks ago. She lives in Wicker Park, Chicago. There's an expired Loyola University student ID card, as well as a Golds Gym membership."

"Must be where she got that killer ass," I mumble, my cheekbone throbbing. I slam the glove box shut. "Outside of a flashlight, fast food napkins and some flavored lip glosses I'd like to taste first hand, there's nothing special in here."

"Bingo," O'Dell waves a handful of notes in my face. "Love letters from Bobby boy. Looks like he'd been stalking her for a while."

"That would explain her desire to blow him up. I guess it's time for a talk."

"Yep."

We enter the house together as Dem throws protective cups at our heads. "I figured you could use those."

"Fuck you," I chuckle, tossing the cup on the table.

"Is she still bound?" O'Dell asks.

"I assume so. I haven't been in there yet, but she was hopping around, banging herself against the door. She's been quiet since you rolled up, so expect an ambush when you open the door."

I sneak a peek at my face in the mirror, my eye already a gorgeous shade of purple. "Fuck."

"There are peas in the freezer, Diva." Dem laughs and shakes his head.

"Grab a bottle of water for her while you're at it." O'Dell takes off his holster and pulls the knives strapped to his thigh out of their sheath. "I'm going in."

I slap the bag of peas on my face and grab the water, walking toward the bedroom as O'Dell says in his deep baritone, "Settle down, Cupcake, or I'm going to tie you spread eagle to the bed."

I walk in behind him with a big smile on my face. "Mmmm, spread eagle. Can we do that anyway?"

She flops on the bed, her eyes narrowing on me. "How's your eye?"

"You've got a beauty of a right hook," I say with genuine appreciation.

"You should try my left," she smirks.

My grin turns wolfish as I let my eyes trail over every inch of her. "Are you offering me a taste?"

Her lips thin, our playful banter over—for the moment. "Come near me and I'll divorce you from your nuts."

O'Dell sighs. "That's enough foreplay. What's your story, Kyra?"

Using her name takes the wind out of her sails. "What?"

"You just blew up three months' worth of surveillance, so start talking about who you are and why you did what you did."

Her head swivels back and forth, taking both of us in. "Surveillance? Are you telling me you're not employed by that asshole?"

"Bobby Lash? How do you know him?" O'Dell keeps the interrogation going.

She huffs. "Are you going to answer one of my questions?"

"No."

"Can you at least untie me?"

"Are you going to continue to fight us?" He cocks an eyebrow.

Her eyes slide my way, and I swear there's a sparkle behind them. Goddamn. Everything about this woman turns me on. "I'll be good—for now."

O'Dell motions to me.

I push her backward, her bound ankles coming off the ground. Untying them first, I then roll her over, working on her cuffs at the same time, putting my mouth near her ear. "I wish we'd met you under any other circumstances. We could have had a lot of fun."

"Knock it off." O'Dell rolls his eyes, his massive arms crossed over his chest. "Spill the deets, Kyra."

She sits up, and I hand her the water. Taking a quick drink, she fills her mouth and casts her blue eyes in my direction, as if she's contemplating spitting at me. I stay close, my lips curled in a small smile, silently daring her to tempt me into a good time.

Swallowing, she moves her eyes back to O'Dell. "Bobby Lash is a human trafficking piece of shit."

"We know that. How do you know that? Or, more importantly, who do you work for?"

"Work for?" She shakes her head, her brow furrowing. "I'm a bartender at night and a receptionist for a mid-sized company during the day."

"Then why have you been casing Bobby's shit shack for the last two weeks?" I ask.

Her eyes shift from me to O'Dell and back to me. "Who are you?"

Changing tactics, I sit on the edge of the bed and try to appear relaxed. "How's your head? Any headaches from the blast? Do we need to worry about a concussion?"

Kyra gives me a placating smile. "My head is fine, but I'm sure I've got bruises from being tackled to the ground not once, but twice, by a guy who has fifty pounds on me."

I lift the hem of my T-shirt and pat my eight-pack. "Fifty pounds of sexy muscle."

She rolls her eyes. "Are you always so obnoxious?"

"Yes," O'Dell grumbles. "He is."

My tactics work. She pushes back on the bed, putting her back against the corner and sighs. "I met Bobby a few months ago at my bar. I served him a couple of drinks and, at the time, he came across as a charming guy. He asked me out for dinner that weekend. Dinner was weird. He was cryptic about himself, refusing to give me any straightforward answers about what he did for a living, where he grew up, his background—everything. However, he was super curious about me. My family, my friends, my support network, etcetera. By dessert he'd thoroughly creeped me out and I knew I'd never go out with him again, but he had other ideas."

"He stalks you." O'Dell pulls the pages out of his side pocket and tosses them on the bed next to her.

She glances at the pages and nods, the first sign of exhaustion causing her shoulders to sag. "It started small at first. Texts and phone calls. Showing up at the bar on my nights off. Then he somehow figured out where I worked during the day and where I live. Flowers at the office, dinners delivered to my home, love notes left on my car windshield. I tried to explain to him I wasn't in a good place for a relationship, but he didn't care. He started love bombing me, getting more and more pushy about us being together, waiting for me at my car at night... stuff like that. We have security on Friday and Saturday nights at the bar, otherwise it's not busy enough to justify the extra staff, but one bouncer, Jimmy, figured out what was going on and stepped up for me, claiming we were together. I didn't hear from Bobby for a couple of days and thought it was over. The next Friday, Jimmy didn't show up for work. On Saturday, I found out he was in the hospital. He'd been jumped on his way to the bar and nearly beaten to death. That night, I got another bouquet at the bar with this note." She holds it up for me to take.

I read the words, a chill skittering up my spine.

LOVE ME OR HATE ME, KYRA—EITHER WAY, YOU'RE MINE. I'VE TRIED MAKING YOU LOVE ME,

BUT I CAN LIVE WITH YOU HATING ME. UNDER-
STAND, I WILL NEVER GIVE YOU UP AND YOU'LL
DIE BEFORE I LET ANOTHER MAN HAVE YOU. IF
YOU THINK YOU CAN RUN FROM ME, I DARE YOU
TO TRY. I KNOW HOW TO MAKE PEOPLE DISAP-
PEAR. USUALLY I SELL THEM OFF, BUT I'LL
KEEP YOU FOREVER. I HAVE AN UNDERGROUND
BUNKER SPECIFICALLY DESIGNED FOR YOU TO
CALL HOME, WHERE NO ONE WILL EVER FIND
YOU. SEE YOU SOON.

"When did you receive this?" I hand the note to O'Dell, anger simmering in my belly. I'm going to tear this asshole limb from limb, videotaping it so I can replay each scene over and over. Actually, I'll kill him slowly, keeping him conscious so he can watch the videos with me.

I might even make us popcorn.

"Three weeks ago." She presses her lips together and says again, "three weeks ago."

I exchange a glance with O'Dell. The look on his face is placid, which means he's just as pissed as me.

Poor Bobby Lash.

Regardless of what Townsend does to us because of our failed mission, something tells me Bobby's days are numbered.

ENTES TUERE
PUNIRE IMPIOS

Chapter Three

KYRA

THESE GUYS—DESPITE the fact they chased, tackled, restrained, pulled my hair, and, in essence, kidnapped me—seem okay. I assumed they were Bobby's hired guns, but judging by the looks on their faces after reading my note, I feel confident they hate him almost as much as I do.

Receiving Bobby's note three weeks ago shook me to my very core. That, coupled with seeing Jimmy in the hospital, and I knew what I had to do. I had to get to Bobby before he got to me.

This isn't my first time with this shit. I was stalked and raped twice by the same guy, right after I dropped out of college. I met him while attending classes. We went out a couple of times, but the chemistry wasn't there —at least not in my mind. He wouldn't take a polite no as an answer, so I ghosted him. I thought he'd moved on because it was months before I ran into him again, in downtown Chicago of all places. Then, his pursuit stepped up a few notches, and he became obsessive. He's still in jail today, but he's eligible for parole next year.

That was seven years ago, and now I'm a black belt in karate. I met an amazing woman who trains SA survivors on how to protect themselves.

Be vigilant. Be smart. Be prepared.

Sadly, I'm not her only student or even her star pupil, because unfortunately, Chicago has plenty of predators and victims to go around.

I eye the two men before me. The guy standing up is broad, maybe six foot two, with dark, close-cropped hair and a beard. His chest and biceps are a work of gladiator fantasies, and the way he stands with his legs slightly spread gives off a confident, but not arrogant vibe. Strong, dominant, imposing—all the things that make most girls' legs go weak.

They certainly do mine.

The guy sitting next to me oozes arrogance, but he does so with a smile on his face—as if us tumbling in the field and him taking a punch to the eye were all part of the foreplay. He's got longer sandy blonde hair on top and his face is normally shaved clean—if the five o'clock shadow is anything to go by. I'd say he's a few inches taller than the guy standing up, but he's leaner and cut, as his eight-pack abs attest. He's the guy you try to ignore at the bar and end up falling into bed with anyway—questioning all your life decisions in the morning. A hell of a lot of fun, but not someone to take seriously.

"Are you going to tell me who you are?" I glance from one to the other.

They exchange a look but say nothing.

"Okay, well, this has been fun, but if that's all, I'll be on my way."

"I'm sorry, Kyra, but you aren't going anywhere," the big guy says.

"Am I under arrest?"

"By us, no. But I'm sure the Feds are going to want to talk to you. You did blow up a house," the guy sitting next to me says.

Another guy pops his head into the room. His eyes spark to life when they land on me. One look at his face and all the air vacates my lungs. He's beautiful in a runway model kind of way. His skin is darker than the other two—his hair too—but his eyes are a mesmerizing golden green.

"Hey," he says.

"Hi."

"I'm Dem."

"Kyra."

He blinks rapidly to break the spell between us and then looks at the big guy that is standing up. "EMS is on site and the flames are controlled. I give them another thirty or forty minutes. What did you tape to the propane tanks?"

"Fireworks."

Dem looks at me with a raised brow. "Fireworks?"

I shrug. "I'm not an explosives expert. I wanted to scare Bobby, not kill him. Hurting someone is the last thing I want to do. I figured he'd come to the house and the heat would be out because the gas was out. He'd see sticks that look like dynamite strapped to the propane tank, know someone was trying to kill him and spend his time focused on the threat to his life and not on me."

"So, you weren't trying to blow up the house?" The hottie sitting next to me quirks his brow.

"Do I need a lawyer?"

Dem chuckles. "We're not cops."

"Who exactly are you?" I point to the other two. "They won't tell me."

He frowns. "You haven't introduced yourself to the woman who gave you that beautiful black eye?"

"Fuck you." The guy sitting next to me offers me his hand. "I'm Kerr. This is O'Dell. We're private contractors working on a joint operation with the Feds. We've had the house under surveillance for months, waiting."

"Waiting? Waiting for what?" Now I'm angry. I've only been tracking Bobby for two weeks and I had already watched him pick up a girl—if she was eighteen, she was a day—and bring her to this house, watching her leave with someone else. It doesn't take a rocket scientist to figure out what's going on in this house. "How many women has Bobby run through that house in the months you've been *watching*?"

All three men look away from me, shame painting their demeanors, deconstructing their confidence.

"That's what I thought."

"Look, Bobby is a layman—a henchman with one specific job in a much larger organization," Kerr says gently. "It's been torture watching and doing nothing more than reporting to the authorities who pick and choose who they save, but Bobby is our ticket to the head honcho. He's desperate to prove himself and move up the ranks, and while Bobby boy is a piece of shit, we need him to get to Joey DiFallo."

I shake my head. "I don't know who that is."

"It doesn't matter. With the house gone, our job is done. We'll head back to Chicago tonight," O'Dell says.

"How'd she blow up the house if she didn't set a trigger?" Dem looks at his two friends, effectively eliminating me from the conversation.

Not that I have an answer, but when they all turn to me, I shrug and spill the details. "I researched online how to *drain* a propane tank by damaging the pressure valve to let all the gas leak out. To hasten the process, I opened all the burners on the stove and then cracked a couple of windows so the gas would vent out."

"Did you turn off the heater?"

"No?" I frown at O'Dell. "Why would I do that?"

They smile, obviously figuring it out before I do. "The open windows cooled down the house. Then the heater kicked on. The electronic ignition provided a spark to a house full of gas. Kaboom. It's actually kind of brilliant—no incendiary device."

"No evidence except for the fireworks," Dem says. "I don't suppose you used gloves when handling them?"

"For the most part, I think so."

"For the most part?" O'Dell leans his back against the wall, crossing his ankles.

"I think so?" Kerr piles on.

I roll my eyes. "I'm not a criminal mastermind, you

know? I didn't expect to blow up a house. I might have touched them at the fireworks stand, or handled the duct tape without gloves, but I was wearing gloves when I taped them to the propane tank. I don't know what else to tell you."

Dem shakes his head. "The tank didn't blow, but it caught fire. We'll have to check it out tonight when we go clear the cameras. Maybe we can collect the evidence before forensics does?"

"Have we called this in?" O'Dell asks Dem. "Maybe we can get the Feds to persuade local LE to slow-roll their investigation."

Dem nods. "They know the house exploded, and that it was empty when it did. I neglected to mention our mystery guest. I figured that could be a surprise for later. They expect us to do a bit of investigation as we scrub the scene before heading home. I'm leaving the call to Townsend to you, our fearless leader."

"Fuck," O'Dell grumbles, pushing off the wall and pulling his phone out of his cargo pocket. "This is going to be painful."

I watch as he walks out of the room. "Now what?"

Dem exchanges a look with Kerr. Jesus, how do these guys do that? With one look, they speak telepathically. It's fucking frustrating. Then Dem gives me a friendly nod and walks out of the room, leaving the door open.

Kerr smiles, scooting back to lean his shoulders against the wall, mimicking my posture. "So, Kyra. You're quite the fighter. It takes a lot to stand toe-to-toe with me, and you definitely did. Where do you train?"

"Penelope Pemshaw is my Sensei."

"Ms. Pemshaw? She's really good." The look on his face tells me he knows exactly who she is and what she's known for, which also means he knows why I'd train with her.

I square my shoulders, uninterested in his pity. "Yeah, she is. She taught me how to give you that pretty black eye."

He grins and damn—he has a sexy smile. It's full of promise and intention. "I'll wear it like a badge of honor."

I glance down at my body, only now realizing it's covered with dead grass and dirt. "I guess you guys aren't going to let me go home?"

Kerr shakes his head.

"Can I at least clean up? I have a bag of workout clothes in my car."

Narrowing his eyes, he stands up and offers me his hand. "Sorry, I shoved your face in the dirt."

"Sorry I threatened to divorce you from your nuts."

His aqua eyes sparkle, but he dips his head, leading me out of the bedroom into a small hallway. "I'll go get your bag. You can wash up in there."

"Thanks."

I close the door behind me, noticing there is no window that could aid in my escape—not that I have my car keys anyway—and resign myself to my immediate fate.

Will they turn me over to the authorities? Probably. How can they not? Of course, they haven't told anyone else about me yet—at least that's what Dem said. I wonder why not? They said they are private contractors working on a joint federal operation, but what does that even mean?

There's a knock on the door. "Your bag, Kitten."

Kitten? Something warm ignites in my belly as I open the door. "Thanks."

"Here are some towels, too. In case you want to take a shower," Kerr offers me clean towels and then takes a step back. "We'll be in the living room when you're ready."

Ready? Ready for what?

I close the door and rifle through my bag, finding my collapsible baton and knife missing. Well, damn. Not that I feel the need to use them against these three, but I hate not having them. They are kind of like my security blankets. Fighting isn't going to stop my future introduction to law enforcement. I mean, I did blow up a house, so I guess I deserve whatever punishment is coming my way.

I strip off my clothes and look at myself in the mirror. There are bruises on my arms and legs, random patterns that look no worse than a vigorous afternoon sparring at the dojo. There's a red mark around my neck, probably from when O'Dell wrapped his big meaty hand around my throat, and there are dirty smudges and a few scrapes on my cheeks and hands. Nothing that won't heal quickly. Considering I could've blown up while dicking around inside the trailer, I suppose I should be thankful these guys chased me out of there when they did.

Good god. I should be dead right now after doing something stupid like trying to scare Bobby into leaving me alone. That certainly puts a new spin on my situation.

These three sexy strangers saved my life, whether they meant to or not.

I guess I should say thank you.

But I'll wait to see if they turn me over to the Feds before I issue my gratitude.

ENTES TUERE
PUNIRE IMPIOS

Chapter Four

I WAIT for the water to turn on in the bathroom, confident she's not eavesdropping at the door, before I turn to Kerr—a man I have known for over thirteen years —and say, "Holy shit, she's beautiful."

"Duh," Kerr says from his position on the couch, his M4 and a cleaning kit laid out on the table. "Why do you think I've been jerking off to her for the last two weeks?"

"Because you're a pig," I point out. "And we've been stuck in the boonies for too fucking long with no relief."

He shrugs. "That's true, on all fronts."

"There's no way you could tell from our video surveillance what she actually looks like. You just got the basic shape of her body."

"Which is phenomenal, by the way. She's got a great ass."

I snort from my seat in front of the video monitors. "I like her because she almost kicked your ass."

Kerr's smile falls. "She's one of Pemshaw's students."

"Penelope Pemshaw?" I raise my brow. I know what that means—we all know what that means. She only picks up sexual assault survivors, teaching them the tools they need to protect themselves from future attacks.

"The very one. Add in a psychopath stalker like Bobby Lash and Kyra has had some shitty luck with men."

O'Dell comes into the living room from the back bedroom and plops down on the couch.

"What's the word?" I ask.

"Scrub the scene, pack up, head home. We have a nine o'clock at the office."

"What did he say about her?"

O'Dell glances between the two of us. "He didn't."

"What do you mean?" Kerr asks.

O'Dell shrugs. "He left it to us until tomorrow. I don't think his initial report to the Feds will include her."

"You know... she was wrong to think this little stunt would deter Bobby. If he thinks his life is in danger, he's smart enough to know that DiFallo will cut him out and tie up any loose ends. Bobby's next move is to run and if he's nearly as obsessed with Kyra as these love notes lead us to believe, he'll want to take her with him."

"She won't go into protective custody," Kerr grumbles.

"Maybe she'd be willing to hang out with us for a couple of weeks until we can lock Bobby down."

They meet my bright idea with silence, my partners side-eyeing each other.

"Locking ourselves up in the house with her is a bad

idea. We all know I want to fuck her," Kerr looks at me. "I saw the sparks between the two of you as soon as y'all made eye contact, so I know you want to fuck her. How are you feeling below the belt, O'Dell?"

"Warm and tingly."

I roll my eyes. "What are we, animals? We can keep our shit together for a couple of weeks while protecting a woman."

"I'm telling you, she's not going to be down with our protection. This chick has fought hard to feel safe on her own. She's not going to appreciate three alpha males beating their chests and pounding their fists on the ground to protect their woman," Kerr grumbles, throwing down an oiled rag.

Their woman. There it is. We're claiming her without knowing what she thinks about us.

"Well, I guess we'll have to see what Townsend says tomorrow, but I don't like the idea of leaving her on her own," I retort.

Kerr nods, sliding the charging handle and bolt in before locking his M4 in place. "Agreed. One way or another, she's getting our protection until we can put Bobby down."

O'Dell nods. "Agreed."

The shower water turns off, so I lower my voice. "I'll put a tracker in her car and then we'll insist she help us scrub the scene. One of us will have to follow her home, all stealth like, but I think we should give her the option of protection, just so she knows it's there."

Kerr and O'Dell exchange another look and nod their heads. "That's a good idea."

"Do we know where Bobby boy is right now?"

I pull up an app on my tactical tablet. "His truck is parked in that crap-hole apartment building, but his Cadillac is on the move in downtown Chicago. I wonder if he's heard about the house blowing up?"

O'Dell shakes his head. "They deeded the house to a shell company, so he wouldn't be the one to get the call. Man, I'd love to be a fly on the wall of that fucking conversation."

I shrug. "Maybe we can be. Let me call Soren."

Kyra comes out of the bathroom in a pair of well-worn sweatpants and a baggy sweatshirt with the neck cut out—giving me serious Flashdance vibes. Her red hair is wet and she's scrubbed her face clean, allowing her skin to glow. She's so fucking touchable, her soft skin begging to be caressed.

Kerr is right. I definitely want to fuck her.

Her gaze swings around the room, meeting each of us in the eye, but she saves her smile for me. "You were right. That shower felt amazing."

"Are you badly bruised?" Kerr asks, and I can hear the regret in his voice.

"Nothing that won't heal," she sits cross-legged in the lone armchair, the neck of her sweatshirt slipping off her bare shoulder.

I turn back to the monitors as the last EMS truck's tail lights turn on and the team pulls off the property. "We're clear."

O'Dell speaks. "So, Kyra. I spoke to our boss and we're not going to hand you over to the Feds just yet. We need you to help us scrub the scene, in case you think of something we miss that could be traced back to you and then..."

I'm unplugging the computer monitors and powering down our computer equipment when O'Dell trails off. Spinning around in my chair, I find her staring at them with her eyebrows arched. "And?"

"We feel it's not safe for you to return to your normal routine while Bobby is running wild."

She frowns. "Why not?"

"The DiFallos aren't going to have a lot of love for Bobby after one of their houses, the one he was assigned, blew up. They won't trust him with another and they might even put a hit out on him to clean up the mess. The house is now public, even if the local LE knows nothing about what has been going on there. DiFallo won't stand for it and we believe Bobby is smart enough to know he's fucked. Therefore, there's a strong possibility he'll come for you on his way out of town."

To her credit, she doesn't immediately dismiss our concern, mulling over things in her head. I rise from my seat and approach, her soft blue eyes coming up to meet mine as I kneel beside her chair. "We have full confidence you can protect yourself. You nearly kicking Kerr's ass proves that."

This causes her to smile while Kerr grumbles behind me. "But we have years of experience with unstable people and Bobby's love notes cause us concern. Don't dismiss how dangerous he can be."

"Or how desperate he will be after this," O'Dell adds.

Kyra lays her hand on mine. "I appreciate your concern. I really do. But one thing I promised myself after the last time this happened was I would never allow some asshole to scare me to where I had to disrupt my life. I refuse to give up my power or freedom."

She looks at each of us, as if to stress her point. "I'm not hiding from him. I'll be vigilant, I'll be careful, but above all, I'll be prepared if he comes for me."

I sigh, recognizing a woman who will not be swayed. Glancing at my partners, they nod, but the gleam in their eyes tells me we're moving on to plan B.

"I guess it's time to go," O'Dell slaps his thighs and stands. "Pack up the necessities. We'll come back next week to dismantle everything else."

I'm the unofficial tech guy of our team, so I return to pulling and wrapping computer cables, throwing them in a box next to the desk. I'm not a Soren—nobody is a Soren except Soren—but I'm the most comfortable of the three of us with computers and all the tech gadgets he shoves in our direction. The man is a genius. Recruited by all the three-letter agencies for his brilliance, but— lucky for those of us employed by the Townsend Security Agency—his brain is better suited for PsySpecOps warfare. Plus, he's bonded with his teammates, Reese and Caiden—not dissimilar to my brotherly bond with O'Dell and Kerr—so he would never leave them.

And now they have a fiancée, a soon-to-be bride. Definitely in it together for life.

Kerr grabs his weapon and all the cleaning gear, walking into the back bedroom where the rest of our arsenal is secured. It takes about twenty minutes to pack up everything important. Weapons, military-grade tech gear, and personal items. Computer monitors and keyboards mean nothing should someone break into the house while we are gone.

It's a couple of hours after sunset when we brazenly pull our vehicles onto the property, making quick work of removing the half-dozen cameras we have hidden in the trees surrounding the trailer. Thankfully, the fireworks ignited, incinerating the duct tape and hopefully any other evidence linking Kyra to the crime scene. We're on the road a half-hour later, Kerr following Kyra in one SUV while O'Dell and I head back to our house in another.

"Should we ask her out?" Kerr says over the phone, which is on speaker through the vehicle's audio system.

"Tonight?" O'Dell shakes his head while gripping the steering wheel.

"No, asshole. Not tonight, but in general."

I shrug, bringing up everything I can find about Kyra Stewart on a database built by Soren—one that taps all the legal and a couple of illegal data mining sites. "We all want her."

"Yes, we do!" Kerr punctuates.

"I don't know. She doesn't strike me as the kind of

woman who would take on a relationship with three men," O'Dell says. "Especially men like us."

"She's too independent?" I can list a dozen reasons why he's right, but I'm curious what his top three are.

"That and she's got some serious control issues."

"Understandably," I point out.

"True."

"That's why she needs men like us," Kerr says. "We'd make her feel safe so she can relax."

"I got to be honest, guys, I'm tired of not having some-one. Ever since Reese, Caiden, and Soren met Leti and Lee, Case, and Porter met Epi, I've been dreaming about the woman perfect for us," I admit my pathetic truth.

But is it pathetic to admit I want a special woman in my life? One that not only understands, but craves the lifestyle my partners and I offer?

"Yeah. Those fuckers have been deliriously happy as of late," O'Dell sighs.

"It's fucking annoying," Kerr agrees.

"Maybe our dream woman isn't Kyra, but I have a feeling about her. The moment our eyes met, this ball of need tumbled around in my gut."

"It's called a hard-on," Kerr quips.

"It's more than that, Oinky."

"Oink. Oink," Kerr jokes, his go-to mode when feel-ings are discussed. I love my brothers, but Kerr bottled up his feelings when he was a kid and hides his wants and desires behind dick jokes and hot sex. I have to give him that—the man is super passionate in the bedroom, channeling all of his feelings into the way he ravishes his women—and sometimes, our women. O'Dell is the more dominant of the three of us, although we all have a slightly sadistic streak. I'm not into inflicting pain, but I love edging—both for her and for myself.

The guys like it, too.

"Oh, shit," Kerr growls. "Shit, shit, shit."

"What?" O'Dell asks.

"I've been made. She literally parked at the red light and is walking past four cars toward me."

I chuckle. "We knew she was smart."

"You suck at tailing," O'Dell adds.

"Hey, Kitten," Kerr says as he rolls down the window, the city traffic coming through the speakers.

"Are you really going to pretend like you aren't following me?" Kyra snaps.

"We never said we wouldn't follow you. You don't want to hide with us, but we're sure as shit not going to lose track of you, especially while Bobby is loose," Kerr responds matter-of-factly.

Cars are honking their horns, so I'm guessing the lights have turned green.

"It'll be faster if you just accept this is going to happen, Cupcake," O'Dell says, letting her know we're listening.

She growls. "You guys are pains in the ass—you know that?"

"Yeah," we say simultaneously.

Kerr chuckles as he rolls up his window, the street noise dying down to nothing. "Oh man, she's pissed."

"If we decide to make a play for her after this is over, we agree now. No one touches her until we all do."

Kerr sighs. "Fine."

"Agreed," O'Dell nods.

Now all we have to do is find Bobby Lash, get rid of him, and then we can make a play for what I hope is our future.

ENTES TUERE
PUNIRE IMPIOS

Chapter Five

KERR

I FOLLOW Kyra a couple of blocks to her apartment, no longer hiding my intent. She already busted me, so fuck it. I exit my vehicle before her, walking over and opening her door, only after I quickly glance around at the cars parked near her complex.

No trucks. No Cadillacs.

No Bobby Lash—from what I can tell.

She lives in a shit hole, the neighborhood overrun with drugs, so I'm not thrilled with the people hanging out nearby. It's near midnight, so it's hard to think that anyone out on a street corner this late is up to something good.

I offer her my hand, which she takes, wincing as she stands up.

"Are you in pain?"

"Just sore. You did smack me around a little."

"I never once laid an open palm or clenched fist on you."

"What about pulling my hair or smacking my ass?" She raises her brow, her lips quirked.

"Foreplay?" I grin back at her.

She shakes her head, motioning to the propped open door leading into the apartment building. "I suppose you want to come inside?"

"Yes, please."

Kyra rolls her eyes and grabs her bag, leading the way. I swear she puts an extra swish into her hips just to tease me. Dem often calls me a pig and I suppose he's right in some ways. I'm not the caring, nurturing one of our team. Things get fucked up if my mind gets involved, so I've learned to lead with my dick. I overthink everything—watching and psychoanalyzing a person's every action to where I imagine things that aren't there. Eventually, every comment becomes a slight I have to respond to, and every action is designed to con me out of something that I'd probably freely offer if I wasn't so fucked up in the head.

My overthinking works great against bad guys, but sucks in relationships with women.

I can't even discuss my heart, which died a long time ago.

Connecting on an emotional level is Dem's strength, intellectually is O'Dell's specialty, and mine is the pure physical. I'm a born flirt and usually the one to introduce a woman I've been chatting up and feeling out for the last five minutes to my partners, who, with one look and twenty minutes of conversation, can convince her to act out something she's only ever fantasized about.

We figured out quickly—after completing PsySpecOps training and deploying on our first mission—that our sexual appetites were similar and the idea of dominating one woman together was a lifestyle we wanted to embrace. It took a few years before we realized we weren't special and that sharing one woman is popular amongst the other PsySpecOps teams. Something in our psych profiles says we're perfectly partnered together both on and off the combat field, each one of us accentuating the others' strengths and eliminating our weaknesses.

You'd think that men who share women lack the possessiveness and jealousy of a monogamous vanilla man, but if anything, I'd say we're worse. O'Dell, Dem, and I haven't met that one woman yet—although, maybe we have—but I know that when we do, we'll be just as territorial over her as Reese, Caiden, and Soren are over Leti.

Or Lee, Case, and Porter are with Epi.

Once we meet our woman, we'll be just as possessive.

She lives on the third floor, in the second-to-last unit in the hallway. She unlocks two deadbolts and the lock in the handle and then hits a button on a key fob, an audible beep coming from her apartment.

"Security system?"

Kyra nods. "Homemade. It's hooked up to a wireless power switch which turns on and off with the press of a button."

"Smart."

She shrugs. "I have my moments."

We enter her apartment, and I grab her forearm gently, pulling her beside me. "Humor me and stay close until we've checked every nook and cranny. Okay?"

Kyra rolls her eyes again, something I suspect she will do a lot with me, and sighs. "Okay."

"Walk me through your place."

"There's not much to it. The bedroom and bathroom are back there and from here you see my living room, kitchen, and dining room. The Taj Mahal, I know, so try not to get lost."

I lean over and check behind the kitchen island, which also functions as her dining table, to ensure no one is lurking under the cabinets. Opening and then closing the small closet near the door, we walk together around the couch and into the bathroom where the shower curtain is pulled back. Last, we check her bedroom, where I look in the closet with the dual sliding doors.

I kneel to check under the bed when Kyra squeaks, "Don't look under there."

"Why? Am I going to find a giant dildo?" I grin at her.

Fuck, I'm at the perfect height to bury my face in her pussy. Fucking bro rules ruining all my fun.

"Why? Are you looking to be pegged?" she comes right back at me, matching my sarcasm with her intoxicating sass.

I stand up to my full height, towering over her, and look into soft blue eyes close to my color. "Oh no, Kitten. I only pitch, never catch."

She licks her lips, staring up at me with a look that dares me to kiss her. "What now?"

Goddamn, I want her.

I take a step back, effectively backing down from her challenge. "Show me your security system."

The muscle between her eyebrows tightens to match her frown. "Okay."

For the next ten minutes, she shows me the locks on her windows, the bullhorn attached to a siren connected to wires attached to the front door, and lastly, her Glock 23 with an extended magazine she has tucked under the bed right next to a box of sex toys. She also has a stun gun hanging from a hook near her pillow.

These security measures impress me, but they also anger me. I love a smart woman who is prepared for anything. I'd love to tumble around with her on a mat and teach her a few new moves—and in this case, I mean that in a non-sexual way. But knowing she had to do this to make herself feel safe after being attacked in the past makes me want to gut a motherfucker.

I wonder if she'd tell me who he was?

He could not breathe anymore.

I wouldn't lose a second of sleep over it.

"This is fantastic, Kyra, but what do you do to protect yourself when you leave the house?"

She sighs, plopping down on a couch that has seen better days. "My most vulnerable time is anytime I leave my apartment or car. I know this. Outside of being vigilant, looking both ways before I walk across a parking lot and having my keys in my hand—" she flashes me a self-defense keychain shaped like a cat's face, "—I don't know what else to do. I can't stop living my life. I refuse to become a shut-in."

I sit next to her, throwing my arm behind her shoulder on the top of the cushion. "We know you can take care of yourself, but we can't, in good conscience, leave you to the wolves. How hard are you going to fight our protection?"

"What kind of protection are you talking about, Kerr?"

"Bare minimum, we'll watch over you until we secure Bobby. Give us a couple of days to clean up the mess you made—" I give her a pointed look, "—and get new orders regarding Lash. We'll either secure him for the Feds, or we'll get rid of him. Either way, he'll never mess with you again. Don't make our job of watching over you hard."

Kyra crosses her legs, her foot brushing up against my calf. "How do I make it *not hard*?"

"Well—" I glance down as she slides her hand onto my knee. My cock immediately jumps to life in my pants with this one simple touch. "What are you doing?"

She smiles, swinging her leg on top of my thigh. "If you're hinting you need to stay the night to protect me, you might as well climb on top and keep me covered."

"Oh fuck," I groan, pushing her leg off mine to stand up.

Kyra giggles. "Are you playing hard to get? I thought everything earlier was foreplay?"

"Oh, I really hope it was, but I can't do this with you

tonight," I adjust my hardening cock. "No matter how badly I want to."

Her eyes drop to my crotch, blatantly checking me out. "Do you think Dem would want to cover me?"

If she's trying to make me jealous, that's the wrong guy to do it with. "I know he would."

"So that's it? You won't because he wants to and you won't risk losing his friendship."

"No, that's not it," I wave my hands and take another step back. "It's complicated. We're not like normal men."

Kyra stares at me for a full minute, reading into every word, searching for an answer. "The three of you share women—don't you?"

Fuck me. If I could convince her to come home with me right now, we could kill two birds with one stone. The best way to protect her is to have me inside her. Can't get much closer than that. "If you really want the answer to that, it's a discussion for the four of us."

She rolls her eyes and stands up. "Fine. You're welcome to sleep on the couch if you feel the need to sleep here."

"I think you're safe enough here, but take our numbers and call in sick to work tomorrow. Give us until the afternoon to plan. Then we'll talk about what the next few days look like. Okay?"

"Let me grab my phone," she walks into her bedroom and pulls her cell out of her bag. Dem already put a tracker in her car, so if she moves, we'll know it, but I also want to track her phone. Luckily, I don't need a chip for that.

She hands me the phone. "Do you want to punch in your numbers?"

"I can do that," I text myself, Dem, and O'Dell and then program in our names. Pulling my phone out of my pocket, I click on one of Soren's homegrown tracking apps, immediately transferring all of her settings to include her MAC address and IMEI number.

"Here you go," I hand it back to her. "Lock up tight behind me and wait for our call tomorrow."

She drags in a deep breath through her nose and slowly lets it out. "I blew up a house today. That's pretty wild, huh?"

I nod, realizing the full force of what happened today is finally hitting her. Then I remember she's a civilian and maybe she was maintaining a tough demeanor all day because of us, but now she's winding down. "It was."

"I'm lucky no one was hurt."

"Yeah, well, it's over now. Don't beat yourself up about it. As you said, the place was a shit hole used for horrible things, so it needed to go up in flames. Take solace from that and don't worry about the rest. We'll take care of it."

And you, I think, but do not speak out loud.

ENTES TUERE
PUNIRE IMPIOS

Chapter Six

O'DELL

I'M surprised when Kerr stumbles through the house into the kitchen for morning coffee. "I didn't hear you come in last night."

Dem looks up from his phone. "How'd it go?"

Kerr nods. "She's something else. Smart and crafty, she rigged up a homemade security system in her apartment—which is in a shit location, by the way—and has everything locked down. Outside of tapping into her system, which we can't do because it is a closed-loop, we couldn't do much better. She's strapped with what she needs should someone try to break in. It's when she leaves the apartment that she's vulnerable."

"Okay... and?" I hand him a mug of hot coffee, black with two sugars. In a lot of ways, the three of us are like an old married couple. We've known each other for so long that we know what each other likes, dislikes, and can anticipate what the other is thinking—most times. Something is bothering him, outside of the obvious.

"I sent you a text and synced her phone to the tracker app."

Dem nods. "Yeah, I've configured her number to send us alerts when she's on the move."

Kerr takes a deep drink and then sets it down. "I asked her to call in sick tonight and give us the day to come up with a plan, but she never actually said she would."

"What did she say?" I ask.

"Aren't we going to be late?" Kerr checks his watch and slugs back the rest of his coffee.

I exchange a look with Dem and follow suit, putting our coffee cups into the sink. "Yeah, meet you in the car."

We're pulling into traffic and heading downtown toward the Townsend Security Agency, an innocuous office building that would shock the neighbors if they knew what kind of arsenal we housed inside the secure vaults within.

"Alright, man. What happened?" Dem leans forward between the seats, breathing down Kerr's neck.

"She came on to me," Kerr frowns. "Aggressively. Well, more aggressive than I'd expect from her."

"Really? And what did you do?" Dem narrows his eyes.

"Fuck you. I backed away, of course. We have an agreement," Kerr grumbles. "Another reason you didn't hear me come in last night. I had a raging hard-on and a need to punch both of you in the face."

Dem snorts and slides back into his seat.

"I'm not surprised she initiated, considering her

trauma response to her assault," I say, pulling off I-94 into thick city traffic. "She has to be in control of everything."

"Did you guys figure out what happened to her?" Kerr asks.

"Yeah," Dem sighs, crossing his arms over his chest. "Some college boy, Brolin Mann, drugged, raped, and dumped her in the backseat of her car a block from the club where he slipped her the HBG. Even though she knew him from school, she didn't report him since she couldn't remember clearly what had happened, or if she'd given consent. What she ended up reporting was that he'd been harassing her at school—which might be the reason she dropped out. A few weeks later, he broke into her apartment. He beat and raped her over a weekend, telling her she was his to do with as he pleased. He made her say it out loud before he finally left and at that point, he thought he had her beat. Instead of running scared, our girl took more than enough evidence to the police, who put him away for twenty years."

"Twenty years for aggravated assault, rape, and imprisonment?"

Dem shrugs. "His family has money. They tried to buy her off, but she said no."

"Good for her. Please tell me we know where this fucker is?" Kerr grits his teeth, going through all the emotions we went through last night. We're lucky we weren't awake when he got home, because both Dem and I were itching for a fight, too.

"He's south of here at Menard. He's got his first parole meeting coming up next year."

"Oh, he's not making that meeting." My hands tighten around the steering wheel.

My partners don't respond. Instead, we sit in silence for a few minutes, each of us no doubt fantasizing about the pain we'll inflict on Brolin and Bobby someday.

"She's a rock, but she crumbled a little last night," Kerr states, his gaze out the window. "The reality of what she'd done was weighing on her. She didn't say so, but I think she was thankful we followed her home."

"You should have talked her into coming back to our house," Dem throws out.

"Nah," I say. "She needs the praise you gave her. I suspect you commended her on her home security system?"

"I did."

"Yeah, she needs that. Especially from guys like us."

Kerr clears his throat as we pull into the garage under Townsend Agency. "One more thing. When I begrudgingly declined her advance, she asked if it was because Dem wanted her. Then she guessed we like to share women. I told her if she really wanted the answer to that, it would be a discussion for another time."

"Did she seem into it?" Dem asks.

He tilts his head and shrugs. "She didn't seem turned off."

I take in a big breath and let it out slowly while killing the engine. "Well, boys, we have a lot to do before we can act on that. Let's get this meeting over with and then we'll go from there."

"GENTLEMEN," Victor Townsend greets us from the conference room where Reese and Lee both sit. Damn, I guess he called in all his leads.

We walk in and shake hands. "Guess you two are pissed at us."

"Actually," Reese chuckles, "we got to sleep with our fiancées last night, so we're happy. The rest of the team— yeah, you should watch your backs."

Lee grins. "Heard you guys had some fun yesterday."

"Something like that," I plop into a chair.

"That's some makeup job you got going on, Kerr," Lee adds.

Kerr touches his black eye. "Yeah. She got me good."

"I hope it was worth it," Reese grins.

Kerr shrugs. "We're hoping so, too."

Both Lee and Reese raise their brows but drop the conversation when Victor comes back into the room, closing the door behind him.

He sighs as he takes a seat, his hands clasped on the big conference room table. "I had a nice long conversation with the Feds yesterday, letting them know that while we appreciate them paying our exorbitant fee to babysit while they gather enough evidence for their prosecution, we are tired of watching shit-bags commit crimes and walk away unscathed. It goes against our very moral fiber to wait while they waste time making sure all of their T's are crossed and their I's are dotted. Normally, we're hired when they want to avoid the red tape."

"Thankfully, they agreed. With one house burnt, they are confident the DiFallo family will scrub the other houses, which means they have to move now with the evidence they have."

"Thank fucking Christ," Lee mutters my exact sentiments.

"Right," Victor leans back in his chair, eyeing the closed door. "Something else for you to know. Not every shitbag you've had to watch walk away has made it out unscathed. Part of the export business has been running out of New Orleans and Miami and our boys down south have been moonlighting for me—off the books, of course. That's all I can tell you for now, but it should provide you with some solace when you close your eyes at night."

Kerr elbows me. "I guess that's why we haven't seen some couriers come back."

"Exactly," Victor quips.

"Nice," I say. "We'll have to take a trip south and buy the boys a beer."

"I prefer you share a bottle of whiskey at Walder's Ranch," Victor states in a tone that brokers no argument.

"Roger that."

"So, what's our next step?" Reese asks.

"They want a couple more days of surveillance to capture any movement from the DiFallo family as they scrub the scenes. They're going to be standing by as well —actually, their agents are probably already shacked up with your teams—ready to arrest anybody that comes to destroy evidence."

"Oh, Case is going to hate that," Lee grumbles.

Reese nods in agreement.

Victor sighs. "Can't be helped. Otherwise, it's time to come home."

I can feel the anxious energy radiating off my partners sitting next to me. "What about Bobby Lash?"

"What about Bobby Lash?" Victor raises his brows.

I exchange a glance with Kerr and Dem before turning back to Victor. "We want him. The woman who torched the house yesterday deserves to know he's no longer a threat."

Victor closes his eyes for a second. "Lee, Reese, you can return to your teams. Let them know they'll be home before the weekend."

Both men nod and stand, throwing us a pointed look. "You need anything, you know how to reach us."

I nod but say nothing. None of us are stupid. These guys—without knowing who Kyra or Bobby are—understand the desire to right a wrong. They also understand the driving need to protect what is theirs, even if Kyra isn't technically ours.

Yet.

Victor waits until they close the door behind them before addressing us. "You are confident she is not working for the DiFallo family?"

"One hundred percent," I nod and slide him a copy of the note from Bobby to Kyra.

He reads it twice before shaking his head. "The Feds

are going to want to bring him up on charges with the rest of them."

Dem growls. "That could take months, and you know he'll be out on bond. He's not high enough on the food chain to warrant locking down."

Victor puts his hands up, effectively silencing our complaints. He's not only the CEO of Townsend Agency, he's our old commander and a trained PsySpecOps officer himself. "The Feds are going to want to prosecute him. However, Bobby Lash has criminal tendencies and if he gets himself killed while perpetrating a crime—well, there's nothing we can do about that."

In our job, both military and civilian, there are orders explicitly given and orders that are never issued out loud. This would be one of the latter.

"You're off the clock for the rest of the week," Victor raps his knuckles on the heavy wood table. "Probably next week, too. I suggest you enjoy your time off. You guys deserve it."

He stands up and slaps Kerr's shoulder on his way out, chuckling, "That is one hell of a shiner. I can't wait to meet the woman who gave it to you."

I wait for the door to close again, wheeling my chair back so the three of us can huddle up and face each other. "What do you think?"

Kerr grins. "We have trackers on him. I say we pick him up, drive him into the boonies and slit his throat. We'll make it look like the DiFallos did it."

Dem shakes his head. "We can't do that."

"Yes, we can. We happen to be very good at it," Kerr growls.

"Making him disappear won't be very satisfying for Kyra. If we tell her *to trust us that he's gone,* she's now an accessory if shit ever hits the fan. Besides, she wouldn't appreciate us cleaning up her problem. Not at this stage in our relationship. If we want something more with her, we have to do this right," I keep my voice calm, a technique I learned in interrogations overseas.

"So, what then?" Kerr is usually the most excited out of the three of us. Our tall and lean hothead. The man has passion for everything he does, whether it's fighting or fucking.

"Two choices," I lean back in my chair. "We either scoop him up, take him somewhere private and let Kyra decide what she wants to do with him, or we make sure we're within reach and give him a crack at fucking up."

"You want to use her as bait? Are you fucking crazy?" Kerr jumps out of his chair and paces the length of the table.

Dem and I watch him for thirty seconds, letting him work out some of his frustration on the carpet. I arch my brow at Dem, who only shakes his head in response.

"Look, motherfucker," I bark to get Kerr's attention. "You want her. I get that. We all do. But you know better than both of us she can hold her own, and taking him down herself will be a hell of a lot more satisfying for her. She needs this win. She needs to know that we trust her to kick ass, while knowing we have her back. We can't take her control from her. She has to give it to us, and this is how we convince her we are the men for her. The ones she can trust to give her what she needs."

Kerr stops his pacing, closing his eyes and tilting his head to the ceiling with his hands on his hips. He knows I'm right. The painful part is admitting it out loud. "Fine, but we will do this tonight. One way or another, this ends tonight. I don't want to drag this out any longer than necessary."

Dem holds up his phone. "I've been watching Bobby all morning. He's been darting around the city running errands, including going to the bank. Soren flagged his account, and Bobby pulled out ten grand in cash a half-hour ago. I think he knows about the house and probably has a meeting with DiFallo today or tomorrow, which is why he's jack-rabbiting around town now. He'll move on her tonight."

"Great. Let's fucking do this and claim our woman," Kerr looks both of us in the eye.

Yeah, I guess it's definite now.

Kyra is our woman.

I hope she's on board.

ENTES TUERE
PUNIRE IMPIOS

Chapter Seven

KYRA

I WAKE UP AROUND NOON, every muscle in my body screaming in protest. My head is pounding. Not from the blast yesterday—although that explains every other ache and pain—but from the crying fit I had last night.

Good god. I can't remember the last time I let myself bawl.

Once I was safe in my apartment, the reality of the day sunk in. I could have died yesterday and it would have been my own damn fault. If O'Dell and Kerr hadn't chased me out of that house, I know I would've been inside when the heater kicked on, because I had had every intention of ransacking the place.

I'm so fucking stupid... and so damn lucky.

I'm also embarrassed about throwing myself at Kerr last night. If I'm being honest with myself, I didn't want him to leave. Not because I was scared Bobby would break in, but because I was terrified of being alone with my thoughts—and rightfully so, considering I cried in the shower until the water ran cold.

When I caught Kerr tailing me on the streets of Chicago last night, I felt a wave of relief wash over me— not that I would ever admit that to him. And yes, I would've loved having him in my bed. He would have been a welcomed distraction, because let's face it, he's hot.

They all are.

I threw out the sharing comment on a whim, but the look on his face told me I was one hundred percent on point. I didn't know that existed outside of porn. What would being shared by three men be like? It seems overwhelming, but in the best possible way.

I squeeze my thighs together, but that hurts, just like every other part of my body. Stumbling out of bed, I pop eight hundred milligrams of ibuprofen into my mouth before starting my coffee pot.

Once my coffee is brewed, I make myself an extra-large mug with frothed cream and settle onto my couch to check my phone. I have three missed text messages, one from each man who saved my life yesterday.

> Kerr: Good Morning, Kitten. I hope you're not too sore today. If it makes you feel any better, my eye looks ridiculous. I will get a bunch of shit about it at the office.

He sent me a selfie and his eye does look bad. I respond with:

Awww, poor baby. Would you like me to kiss it better?

O'Dell: It was interesting meeting you yesterday, Cupcake. I hope the next time we meet, it will be under better circumstances. We'd like to spend more time getting to know you. Stay safe and vigilant today. If you need anything from us, we're one call away.

I respond with:

I'd like to get to know you, too, but without the explosions and near-death experience.

Finally, I got a sweet note from Dem.

Dem: I hope you slept well, Angel. We didn't get nearly enough time together, but I can attest you were the best part of the last three months in that hellhole. If you need us, we'll be there. Don't be afraid to call us for anything.

He sent me a gif of a kitten snuggling with three puppies. It's so corny that it's cute and definitely gives me ideas.

I respond with:

Am I the kitten? That's what Kerr keeps calling me.

Dem: You are definitely the kitten, although I prefer to think of you as an angel.

I'm no angel.

Of course, you are. Either that, or an angel brought you to us. I knew it the moment I laid eyes on you.

Yeah, I definitely felt something when our eyes locked yesterday. Almost like I recognized him, even though I would never forget a face like his. It wasn't my brain putting two and two together; it was my heart. But considering I've never been in love, I don't see how that is possible. Maybe it wasn't my heart, but a muscle lower on my body.

For a woman who has been through the shit I've been through, I'm very sex-positive. I refuse to let Brolin's nightmare turn me into a shut-in or a prude. I refuse to let him take a healthy sex life or my self-confidence away from me either.

Of course, everything has to be on my terms.

I fuck who I like, when I like, and when I do, I'm always on top—working for my climax and not really concerned about if my lover gets off.

Is that awful? Maybe, but I've never known a man to complain.

As long as he is kind and respectful, we can have a good time. I've had a few relationships—if you can call them that—with men I've enjoyed. Of course, they only last a few months at a time. Once they become too clingy, I send them packing.

And, obviously, I attract the occasional nut job. I wonder what it is about me that draws guys with obsessive personalities who can't take a hint?

More text messages come in. Two from Kerr, one from O'Dell, and one from Dem.

This is flattering, exciting, and ridiculous. If they really share their women, I suppose a group text is a natural step toward that possibility.

I open a new message, putting all three of them on it.

> Do you realize you're all talking to me at the same time?

O'Dell: Yes

Dem: Yes

Kerr: Yeppers

> Smartasses.

My phone rings, and it's Kerr.

"Yes?" I put extra syrup in my voice.

"How are you feeling, Kitten?" Kerr all but purrs.

"Sore, but thankful I'm alive."

"Are you hungry? We thought we'd bring you some lunch," Dem says.

It's crazy how I can already tell their voices apart. Dem has a gentleness to his tone, as if he's holding the dark and broody at bay. Kerr has a teasing lilt and you can hear the cocky smile playing at his lips. O'Dell's voice is deep and authoritative. I can easily imagine him barking out orders to trembling subordinates.

"Three big men and me in this tiny ass apartment. Are you joking?"

"You can sit on my lap if you need a place to sit."

"Hmmm," I roll my eyes, but can't keep my lips from spreading into my own goofy grin. "I was thinking I'd run down the street and grab a burrito."

"I thought we agreed you wouldn't leave your fortress today," O'Dell says.

"I never agreed to that."

"I know you didn't, Kitten, but I was hoping you'd do it, anyway."

"You don't know me very well, Kerr. I never do what I'm told."

"That's a quick way to get yourself spanked," Kerr says.

I know he's flirting and part of me is desperate to establish a relationship with that kind of trust, but I've halted talk like that for so long, my knee jerk reaction is to shut down and say nothing.

"Kyra? You still there?" Dem asks.

"Yeah, I'm still here. Sorry."

"You want to give Kerr another black eye?" he jokes. At least I think he's joking.

I giggle. "No."

"Can we bring you lunch?" O'Dell cuts in. "Burrito shop on the corner, right?"

I give up. "Yes. Carne Asada with guacamole and Pico, no beans."

"Roger that. We'll be there in fifteen minutes. Anything to drink?"

Might as well go all out. "Horchata."

"You got it, Cupcake. See you soon."

The line disconnects and just like that, I have a lunch date with three men in my crap-hole apartment. Jumping off the couch, I run into the bathroom to brush my teeth and hair, scrubbing my face again before applying moisturizer and a smidge of mascara. I'm putting on a tank top when there's a knock on my door.

For the last couple weeks, I've gone quiet when someone unexpectedly knocks on my door and then a knee-jerk reaction to crouch down and grab my gun takes over my body.

It's like they know what I'm thinking because my phone beeps with a message. *"It's us at the door."*

I open the door, wondering how my apartment complex is still standing with these three massive men hovering in the hallway. "Come on in."

O'Dell hands me a black T-shirt. "Is there a reason this is hanging over the camera above your door?"

I sigh. "Yeah, my neighbor is afraid I'm going to videotape his side piece coming over when his wife's at work. I tried to explain to him it's not a real camera and just up there to deter would-be robbers, but whenever his date comes over, he throws something over it."

"It's not a real camera?"

"No. My landlord told me I'd have to pay for damages if I drilled through the wall to run a cable."

O'Dell frowns and walks past me to the kitchen island.

Dem walks in behind him, flashing me a sweet smile. "Angel."

"Handsome," I reply, wondering what nickname I should give him or any of them. I'll have to think about that.

Kerr walks in and his eye looks even worse than it did in the photo.

"Oh my god," I slap my hand over my mouth. "Did they hit you a couple more times last night, because there is no way I did that to you?"

He smiles. "It looks worse than it feels."

"I hope so."

Kerr lowers his head, so his mouth is near my ear. "I'm sorry if I went too far on the phone, Kitten."

I place my hand on his hard pec, temporarily stunned stupid by the physique this man is rocking underneath his button-down collared shirt. He flashed me his abs yesterday, but every inch of him must be carved out of stone.

"You didn't go too far on the phone, Kerr. You just surprised me, that's all."

His blond hair falls forward over his blue eyes, his stubbled jaw and plump lips so close, I'm tempted to lift on my toes and kiss him. "Look, we know you've been through some shit, so I'll do my best to tone down my flirting. The last thing I want to do is make you uncomfortable."

"I'm not uncomfortable and the last thing I want

you to do is tone down your flirting," I take a small step back and glance over my shoulder at Dem who is watching us from the kitchen island. O'Dell has his back to us and has taken residency at my window, looking down at the street below. "Did you look me up? Read the reports?"

Dem cast his eyes to the small feast they brought me for lunch. "Yeah, we did."

Exhaling a long breath, I roll my shoulders back. "So then, you know how fucked up I am."

He shakes his head. "We don't think you're fucked up. We think you're amazing. You're a survivor, Angel."

"Better than a survivor. You're a fucking warrior," O'Dell growls, glancing at me from over his massive shoulder.

Warrior—damn, I like the sound of that. I also like the way he's looking at me, like he would raze villages to protect me.

"Besides," Kerr slides his hand onto the small of my back, "you're talking to three men who swim in fucked-up-ness. Anything vanilla and normal makes our skin crawl."

"Horchata?" Dem breaks into our conversation by offering me a to-go cup with the straw already in it.

Smart—the conversation's getting a little heavy.

I peruse the food. "Which burrito is mine?"

Dem hands me a paper-wrapped burrito on a plate. "We also picked up chips and salsa, if you want them."

"Wow. Dinner and conversation—this is the best date I've had in a long time," I sit cross-legged on the floor in front of the coffee table, leaving the couch to them. "Are you going to eat?"

Dem and Kerr sit across from me on the couch while O'Dell stands near the kitchen island. It's only now I realize all three of them are wearing slacks and button-down shirts and they look and smell really nice.

"You know, you clean up pretty good. Do you always dress like this when you go into the office?"

"Our boss wants us dressed to impress, in case there are clients in the building. It's this or full tactical gear, nothing in between," O'Dell rolls up his sleeves before unwrapping his taquitos, his forearms heavily tattooed.

I wonder how much more of his body is inked?

I wonder what he would think about my ink?

"Did you get in trouble for my explosion yesterday?"

Kerr and Dem look to O'Dell, who shakes his head. "No. Honestly, the agency was done with the operation and ready to come home. This gave us the push we needed to let the Feds know it's time to wrap it up."

"You did us a favor, Kitten."

I consider their words, taking a couple bites of my burrito, my stomach rumbling from twenty-four hours without food. I didn't realize how hungry I was after yesterday's excitement. The guys also dig into their food and I'm impressed by how clean they are—napkins and all. Meanwhile, a piece of guacamole-covered Carne Asada drops out of my burrito and lands on my chest.

Of course.

I clean myself, glancing up to see Kerr's lips curled in a smile.

I stick my tongue out as a silent response. Then I decide to get to the topic at hand—why they are really here right now?

"What about Bobby?" From what I've learned about these guys in the short time I've known them, I bet they're tracking Bobby and probably know where he is right now.

"Bobby's a problem. The Feds are going to want him as part of their giant prosecution, but we're not willing to wait around for them to figure it out."

"What does that mean?"

"That means, Kitten, if you want us to make him go away, we can do that."

"Are you saying you would kill him for me?"

Kerr shrugs, but says nothing.

O'Dell clears his throat. "We would make the problem go away, and that's all you need to know."

I shake my head. "Why would you do that for me? You don't even know me. I'm nothing to you."

"True, we still have a lot to learn about each other—" Dem captivates me with his gentle voice and dazzling gold-green eyes "—but never think you are nothing to us. You mean more than we can explain."

All the mental armor I wear for everyone else falls off me. I don't know why, but I trust these men with every-thing I have, including my body and my heart.

Who knew blowing up a house would also blow up my entire insulated existence?

ENTES TUERE
PUNIRE IMPIOS

Chapter Eight

DEM

I SEE the moment Kyra drops the last of her guard with us. I don't think she would've done it willingly, but sometimes our souls or spirits or whatever guiding us through life know who we can trust and be ourselves with. Just like I knew the moment I laid eyes on her that she was meant for us.

"I don't want you to *take care* of my problem for me, but I appreciate your willingness to do so," Kyra smiles, although it doesn't quite reach her eyes as she casts her gaze to her burrito. "I will say, your offer is the most romantic thing one man—much less three—has ever made me."

"We take care of what is ours," O'Dell's voice drops an octave, causing her to bring her head up.

She stares at him for a good five seconds before whispering, "I'm not yours."

He arches his brow. "Not yet, but we're hoping to convince you to think otherwise."

"Let us show you how good we could be together." I lean forward with my elbows on my knees, causing her to swing her beautiful eyes my way.

Her gaze shifts to Kerr, who smiles with one eyebrow cocked in challenge as his response.

"How does one woman date three men?"

"From what we've seen, not lightly," O'Dell states, pushing off the island to retake his spot near the window.

She tilts her head. "Are you saying that from experience with prior relationships, or do you know other couples—is that even the right word—who date like this?"

"We know other *families*."

This seems to surprise her. Kyra takes a second to think, the gears in her beautiful head churning. "Why? I mean, why date the same woman?"

"We are men who enjoy being the best at everything we do and we learned a long time ago we are best when we do things as one. Together, you get the best of us—"

"A damn near perfect man," Kerr grins, which causes her to roll her eyes and smile.

I add, "Who will move heaven and hell to give you everything you want—"

"And everything you need," Kerr finishes my thought.

She stands and picks up her plate, walking into the kitchen with her back to us. "So, this isn't a kinky sex thing?"

"Oh, there's definitely kinky sex involved," Kerr replies—because, of course, he would.

She turns around to face us. "How kinky?"

"That would depend on you," O'Dell says evenly. "But we are dominant males, if that gives you any ideas."

She bites her lip. "I see. How do you deal with jealousy?"

"If you were ours, we would have nothing to be jealous of between the three of us. Individually, each one of us has our strengths and weaknesses, just like any man. You'd get what you need from each of us in different ways—we know that about ourselves—which is why we don't get jealous of each other because all we care about is taking care of you." The words flow out of O'Dell like we've practiced this speech a million times.

We have not.

We've uttered nothing close to a woman before, but that's because we've never found one that all three of us wanted for more than one night. "Possessiveness is a different conversation. Men like us are very territorial over what is ours."

"Are you planning to lock me up in a cage?" She chuckles, so I assume she's making a joke, but I want to make sure that we're very clear about our intentions.

I approach the other side of the kitchen island, leaning my back against the wall and crossing my arms over my chest. "We will never, ever, force you to do anything you don't want to do, although we might not give you what you want in the way you want it. We are protective, we are loyal, and we are loving—and yeah, we might be a tad much—but if you ever thought we were being overbearing, all we ask is that you let us explain our rationale before you chew our asses about it."

She turns and rests her butt against the counter, her hands gripping the edge, which makes her round breasts jut out in invitation. "Do you guys give this pitch to all the women who blow up your house?"

"No."

"Then, why me?"

"Because you're smart," O'Dell says from the window.

"Because you're strong—emotionally and physically," I say.

"Because you're fucking sexy," Kerr all but growls from the couch.

A light blush hit her cheeks. "I don't know what to say to that."

"You don't have to say anything, Angel. We weren't planning on talking to you about this today, but you brought it up. We've never had this conversation with a woman before because, as you can imagine, it's difficult to meet someone that satisfies what all three of us desire in a partner. I knew it the moment I laid eyes on you."

"You knew what?"

"You're the one."

Her lips part, and she stares back at me.

Kerr clears his throat. "You knew it too, Kyra. I saw the way you looked at Dem when he walked into the room."

She nods. "There was something."

"I'd like to think we would have felt something if we'd met under different circumstances."

Kyra giggles. "I felt something when you were sitting on my ass, grabbing at my hands."

Kerr grins, his eyes trailing down her body. "Yeah, I felt something, too."

She blushes slightly and shakes her head, turning her gaze to O'Dell, who stands by stoically and says nothing.

"We don't have to talk about this now, Angel. We just want you to know where we're coming from—"

"And why I begrudgingly declined whatever you were thinking last night," Kerr interjects.

She drops her eyes to her hands and I notice she picks at her nails when she's overwhelmed. "I'm going to use the bathroom. Do you need anything to drink before I go?"

"We're good," O'Dell shakes his head, watching as she walks across the tiny living room into her bedroom.

"Well, this is fucking awkward," I grumble.

O'Dell walks back over to the island so we're only a few feet apart and talks low under his breath. "She's not the kind of woman we send Kerr to feel out and then woo for us at the club. He's the one with the best kink radar, always attracting women who are up for a walk on the wild side. Three men at once is pretty wild, even though we are fairly tame compared to our brethren. Since we don't want Kyra for a night, but for a lifetime, this awkward conversation was unavoidable. With her past, she needs to know exactly what we're offering."

"Agreed, but it doesn't make this any less unbearable," I glance at Kerr, who stands and stretches before walking over. "I think we're freaking her out."

Kerr shakes his head. "Nope. She's into it, but she's doing the math, trying to understand how it would work. I wonder what she was going to school for before she dropped out? I bet it was engineering or something technical like that."

"Why do you say that?" We're all trained to read people and profile them, so we can interrogate and manipulate them if we have to, but Kerr is by far the best reader out of the three of us. He's got a sixth sense and walked into the military with it. I think he developed it at a young age to survive growing up in his ever-changing foster homes.

"Because of how her brain works. She's not afraid to ask questions, wanting all the facts before deciding what she thinks. She carefully picks her words, too. Super smart, which also explains her reaction to her rape. No one wants to think of themselves as a victim, but a lot of women self-blame. Think about how we'd beat ourselves up if someone got the drop on us. She feels like she should have been smart enough to anticipate and or avoid her attack, even though intelligence has nothing to do with it. She could have become a shut-in and walled herself off from the world, but she refused and became what I'm willing to bet is a black belt in karate. She's not scared or sexually stunted, but controlled and calculated. She's fucking perfect for us."

"Except we're going to want to take that control from her," O'Dell points out.

"No, we want her to give up control to us, but only in the bedroom, and only when it's the four of us playing,"

Kerr points at me. "Well, he might want it all the time, but that's between him and her."

I change the subject, taking a minute to check my phone. "She doesn't want us going after Bobby, so we either camp out here or convince her to come to our place to play Monopoly or something."

"I vote *or something*," Kerr mutters.

"Meanwhile, I'm going to call our agency contact and ask them what their plans are regarding Bobby," O'Dell also ignores Kerr, pulling out his phone. "Where is he now?"

"He's across town at his apartment. There's been no movement for the last half-hour."

"Maybe he's already dead," Kerr grins.

"We can only fucking hope. All right, I guess I'll go down to the truck and make this call. Be right back," O'Dell makes a move for the door when Kyra comes out of her bedroom.

"Are you leaving?" She looks from him to me and back.

"I'm going to make a call and then I'll be back."

"Quick question before you go," she walks toward him, stopping maybe two feet away, but definitely within touching distance.

"Yeah, Cupcake?"

Her face lights up when he calls her his little pet name, something I've never heard him do before her.

"The three of you are looking for one woman, so if I were to kiss one of you, I'd have to kiss all of you?"

He raises his brow. "You don't have to do anything

you don't want to do. But our bond is very strong and we all want you, so we've agreed not to pursue you individually."

She dips her head and takes another step forward. "That came out wrong."

To my surprise, she jumps up and wraps her arms around O'Dell's neck, pulling him down to claim his lips.

Kerr chuckles next to me, murmuring, "That's our girl."

O'Dell responds quickly, sliding his hands down to cup her ass and pull her against his body. He deepens the kiss and makes her moan, which causes the blood in my veins to rush south.

Kerr, as if he knows what to expect, walks back over to the couch and sits down, casually putting his ankle on top of his knee and draping one arm over the top of the cushion. He looks like a man confidently waiting his turn. Sometimes, I really want to smack the smugness off his face, but now would not be one of those times. I'm too shocked and turned on to give him any shit for being right.

O'Dell finally pulls back to look into Kyra's eyes. He smiles and then whispers something into her ear that not even I, with my supersonic hearing, can pick up in this tiny apartment. She nods and lets him go, taking a small step back, her eyes glued to his. He performs one last caress of her jaw, smoothing his thumb over her bottom lip and then makes eye contact with Kerr and me before walking out the door.

Kyra bites her bottom lip and looks at me. "Well, this

is awkward. Do I come over there, or do you come over here?"

I chuckle. "I was saying the same thing to the guys while you were in the bedroom. This entire conversation has been awk—"

"Sweet Christ, Dem! Kiss the woman before I do," Kerr barks.

We both take a couple of steps towards each other, meeting in the middle. I cup her face in my hands, staring into her stormy blue eyes sparkling with sexual energy. "Are you sure you want to do this?"

"Am I sure I want to kiss you? Yes."

"Yeah, but after you kiss me, you have to kiss Kerr," I wrinkle my nose, acting as if I am disgusted by the idea, which makes her giggle.

Behind us, Kerr grumbles, "You should be so lucky, fucker."

I lower my head and kiss her gently, her bottom lip soft and plump and begging to be nibbled. Kyra runs her hands up my arms until she's sliding her fingers into my short hair, her lips parting to let me get my first taste of her. She brushed her teeth while in the bathroom—probably spending that time debating the pros and cons of getting involved with three men—peppermint mixing with the horchata on my breath. On instinct, I take several steps back until my calves hit the couch cushion, slowly sitting down and coaxing her onto my lap. She kneels on the cushion beside me with her weight shifted so she's pressed against my thigh.

I sense more than see Kerr move on the opposite end

of the couch, both feet planted firmly on the floor as he reaches out and touches her leg.

Pulling back, I kiss and then suck her lip into my mouth. Our eyes locking on to each other. "You are every-thing I want, Angel."

She smiles at me drunkenly, our kiss mutually intox-icating.

Kerr's hand comes into my field of view to caress her cheek and gently turn her face toward him. Suddenly, I'm thankful for her small couch, perfectly built for the three of us, with her nestled in the middle. As he kisses her, her leg is pressed against mine with my hand caressing her upper thigh. She still has her hand on my chest, which drops lower as he dazzles her with his talented tongue—one that I know makes women moan.

It's when she curls her fingertips into my belt that I know Kerr's kisses have driven her out of her mind and this could go from PG-13 to rated X quickly.

ENTES TUERE
PUNIRE IMPIOS

Chapter Nine

KERR

FUCK ME—KYRA tastes like Christmas. It might be the peppermint on her tongue mixing with the chocolate Hershey's Kiss I sucked on ten minutes ago—I have a huge sweet tooth—or it might be the way she's lighting me up from the inside.

If Kyra was nervous, she got over that shit quickly. She's got one hand on Dem's belt, her other hand on my thigh. She gives me control of our kiss, my tongue tangling with hers. It's the middle of the day, on what normally would be a workday for all of us. We're in her tiny apartment that can't possibly contain the things that we want to do with her. O'Dell's not here, so this can only go so far. It's going to take everything within me not to lay her out on the coffee table like a buffet.

I run a line of kisses along her jaw and up to her ear, whispering words of encouragement. "Kiss Dem again, Kitten."

She turns her head, and Dem is right there to claim her luscious lips.

Sliding my hand up her inner thigh, I'm thankful she has pants on. If she was wearing a skirt, there'd be no way I could keep my fingers from slipping inside of her panties.

I want to play with her.

I want to tease her until she's dripping down my hand and soaking my cufflinks.

And then I want to taste her, sucking every drop from my fingertips.

Her fingers curl into my inner thigh, brushing the tip of my growing erection, and it takes all my willpower not to arch my hips up into her touch.

The one thing about me and my partners—none of us are greedy. So, it isn't long before Kyra's turning back to me, our lips sealed again, tongues dancing as my kitten purrs for me.

This time she boldly grabs my cock through my slacks, her fingers kneading the hardening flesh. I can't help but groan and shift my hips, letting her touch me in a way that I've been fantasizing about for weeks.

She must do the same thing to Dem, because he also groans, our fingers meeting at the apex of her thighs. She's wearing yoga pants, the material thin enough to feel her wet heat radiating through the crotch. Kyra unabashedly spreads her knees wider, granting us access —and fuck me, it's the sexiest thing a woman can do. I love it when a woman knows what she wants and has no problem asking for it.

I love it even more when it's my woman.

"Do you want to come, Kitten?" I nod when she looks at me, as if to give her the answer I'm desperate for her to say out loud.

"Yes," she mewls.

"O'Dell should be here the first time you come. He's going to want to see you come apart."

Dem smiles. "Can you hold it for us, Angel? Will you let us tease you, pleasure you, edge you until all three of us are here to make you orgasm?"

"Edge me?"

His smile grows wider. He fucking loves this shit. "Yes, edge you. We'll tease you and bring you to the verge of orgasm and then back off, only to build you up to the edge again—over and over until you fucking can't stand it and beg us to let you come. And then when you release, it'll be one hundred times more powerful than it normally is. You will explode. Your entire body will go numb and tingly, and you'll be flying high as oxytocin rushes through your veins."

Kyra raises her brow. "Is that what you're into?"

"It is."

Then she looks at me. "What are you into?"

I lick my lips. "Everything. But mostly, I'm looking forward to getting a taste of you."

She bites her lip. "This is kind of crazy."

"Kitten, this is only the beginning," I squeeze her thigh, making sure my thumb brushes against her pussy with enough pressure to let her know it's not by accident.

O'Dell walks back into the apartment, takes one look

at us in the position we're in, and shakes his head. "Sorry to bust up the party, but we have work to do."

"No, we don't," I shake my head like a petulant child.

Fuck me! I do not want to walk away from her when we're just getting started.

"Yeah, we do," he chuckles and walks over, offering his hand to Kyra. "Come with me, Cupcake."

She takes his hand, and he easily pulls her into his arms, setting her on a stool in front of the tiny kitchen island. "This will only take a couple of hours. Why don't you clean up and pack an overnight bag? We'll pick you up later and take you to dinner."

"I'm working tonight."

I stand and approach them. "I thought we agreed you weren't going out tonight."

"I already told you, I never agreed to that. I have a bar shift tonight and I cannot afford to take another night off of work. Besides, Thursday is a good night for tips and I need the money to keep up my lavish lifestyle—" she waves a hand over her apartment "—as you can see."

O'Dell dismisses my concerns. "It's fine. We've been tasked to pick up Bobby and turn him over to the Feds. Unless that goes horribly wrong, he'll be off the street in the next couple of hours, anyway."

"Really?" A big smile takes over Kyra's face. "That's fantastic. I hope all the women he's brutalized get justice."

Dem stands up and is also within arm's reach of her. "That's why you didn't want us to take care of him for you—you want him to stand trial?"

She nods. "It would be selfish of me to be the only woman to know he got what he deserved. I have no idea how many women you've seen him run in and out of that place in the last couple of months, but I'm sure he was doing it long before you got involved. All those women deserve justice and unfortunately, prison won't be nearly bad enough for the likes of him."

O'Dell smooths her hair back and tilts her chin up, planting a chaste kiss on her swollen lips. "You're a good girl—thinking of others when you could've had vengeance for yourself. You are way too good for the likes of us, that's for sure."

"I'm sure I'm not."

"We still want you to pack a bag. What time does your shift start?"

"Five o'clock," she glances over her shoulder at a digital clock.

It's one now.

"We should be done before that, and if we are, we'll pick you up. Otherwise, we'll meet you at the bar."

"You trust me to leave the house on my own?" She smirks at no one in particular.

Dem steps between her splayed thighs and cups her face. "It was never a question of trusting you, Angel. It's about us worrying over and protecting you. If Bobby came after you, we don't know he would come alone. I mean, he took down a big bouncer, right? He couldn't have done that on his own."

"That's true." Her features soften as if she realizes something new. "I never thought about that."

"And yet you thought we were his goons?" O'Dell grins.

"Using goons to beat up a big bouncer or protect his slave trading shack differs totally from attempting to kidnap a woman."

"Criminal minds are criminal minds." Dem kisses the tip of her nose. "They rarely have a code of ethics or a line they're not willing to cross."

"Let's get out of here." O'Dell leans in and kisses her cheek again. "We'll see you tonight."

I wait until both O'Dell and Dem are at the door before I move in between her legs, sliding my hands around her ass and pulling her to the edge of the stool. I press my aching cock against her warmth and suck her earlobe into my mouth. "I can't wait to spread you out and lick every inch of you, Kitten. I'm going to bathe your body with my tongue, get you dirty and then lick you clean again."

Kyra's breathing quickens, her chest rising and falling against mine. "Oh, my."

"Mmmm," I kiss her neck. "Can you imagine my tongue sliding along your pussy and flicking against your clit?"

"Ohhh," Kyra closes her eyes and rests her forehead on my shoulder.

"I want you to think about it until we see each other later. Can you do that for me, Kitten?"

"Yes," she moans, grinding her pussy against my cock.

"You're going to be hot and swollen by the time I get my hands on you tonight, aren't you?"

She brings her head up. "I guess you have your own version of edging."

"Yeah, I guess I do." I kiss her lips, aware O'Dell and Dem are growling at me from the door. "Gotta go."

I stop in the doorway and look back at her. She vibrates with sexual energy right now, making her shimmer in my eyes. "No masturbating and no getting off without us. Understand?"

"Okay." She looks drunk on the pleasure we're promising her, and that vision will keep me hard for the next few hours.

"Lock the door." I close it behind me and follow my partners out of the apartment building, satisfied when I hear her deadbolt slide into place.

Seconds later, I'm cursing as I jump into the passenger seat and adjust my cock. "Fuck me."

"You two primed her nicely in my absence," O'Dell says as he pulls into traffic.

"She's fucking perfect. I can't wait to plunge my tongue into her cunt." I glance at my phone, reading a text message with intel that I neglected to pay attention to while kissing her on the couch. "When did we get this?"

O'Dell chuckles at my inability to multitask. "While you were sweet-talking our woman. The Feds are moving on Joey DiFallo's complex in the next two hours. We're on Bobby. Reese and his team are moving on their rabbit, while Lee and his team are on theirs. If everything goes well, they will lock everyone up tonight, and we'll all be cock-deep in our women before morning."

Dem smiles and chucks me on the shoulder. "She's going to be ours."

I nod. "Yeah, I think so, too. She wants us. She's bold enough for the likes of us. But we'll need to convince her how serious we are about the day-to-day aspects of our relationship. Having a couple of weeks off will help. We can take the time to date her, because I don't think she's ever been in a real relationship. She's always kept a wall up, allowing other men to only get *so* close to her. We'll have to break through that wall."

"I'm up for the challenge," Dem says.

I nod as O'Dell says, "Me, too."

We drive to the Townsend Security Agency building, which is on our way to Bobby's shit hole apartment down south. "Has he moved at all?"

"No," Dem frowns. "I wish we had eyes on his place."

"No cameras in the vicinity?"

"None that we've tapped into to date, and Soren is too busy with his own mission to bother him."

"Old school approach, I guess," I jump out of the passenger seat after O'Dell shuts down the engine. We take the elevator up to the second floor where the gym and locker room are and change into our tactical gear. Then we hit the vault, strapping our favorite handguns to our holsters. I'm keen on the Glock, while Dem prefers the Beretta. O'Dell's a purist with his ambidextrous Smith & Wesson. We grab a garden variety of gear, but considering we're entering an apartment complex in a heavily populated neighborhood with no local law enforcement coordination, we'll do our best to remain low key.

Ten minutes later, we're doing last-minute coordination and driving the seven miles to Bobby's apartment.

All three of our cell phones beep, Dem's phone throwing out a lyrical tone. "That's our woman."

> Please be careful. You've made my body promises I expect you to keep tonight.

I grin as I type out our response:

> We are men of our word and nothing short of death will stop us from keeping our promise to you. Nothing.

O'Dell drives past Bobby's apartment building, where we clock both vehicles parked on the street. There are two men talking on the sidewalk, one of them with a pit bull mix on a leash. One building down there are a couple of kids playing outside the doorway, but otherwise, the neighborhood is quiet.

"I'm going to circle around and park on the south end of the street. We'll approach from there," he says.

"You want me to take the backdoor?"

He shakes his head. "Dem will take the window since he's on the first floor. You and I will take the hallway. I'll do the approach. He's really got nowhere to go."

"Roger."

We approach as a unit, Dem ducking down at the corner of the building while O'Dell and I run beneath the windows of the first floor. They propped the door to the apartment building open and we enter without incident, walking down the hallway toward Bobby's apartment. The hallways are quiet, too quiet, which differs from the building next door, which is bustling with activity.

Dem is in our ears. "The two guys with the pit bull are watching, but they're not making a move. Something tells me they are used to seeing law enforcement around here."

O'Dell approaches Bobby's door and then stops, signaling to me there's something wrong.

I inch closer and notice the door has been kicked open, the frame severely damaged. And then we hear the telltale sound of a 12-gauge pump-action shotgun cocking a round.

"Take a step inside and I'll fill you full of holes," a male voice who I can only assume is Bobby calls from inside the apartment.

O'Dell and I both take defensive positions with our weapons drawn. "Did the DiFallo family come to see you today? If so, we're not with them."

"Oh yeah? Then who are you?"

"We're private contractors hired to get you somewhere safe," I say, making sure he understands there are at least two of us out here.

Dem is once again in our ears. "That is definitely a 12-gauge he has trained at the door."

"Put the lasers on him," I whisper.

O'Dell uses his booming voice again. "Bobby Lash—

the only way you make it out of this alive is by putting the gun down. I'm going to swing the door open and if your muzzle is pointing in my direction, my friends outside your window are putting two in your chest and one in your head. If you think I'm lying, look down at the red dots on your shirt."

"Oh shit," Bobby whimpers.

"Listen to me, man. Be smart," I say. "Put the cannon down."

"What are you offering?"

O'Dell shakes his head. "I don't have the authority to offer you dick, but if you come with us willingly, I promise DiFallo won't be gutting and displaying your intestines as an example to the rest of his organization. We know how he takes care of people he thinks are snitches, and since the Feds are moving in on him right now and your house blew up yesterday, he's going to think you're the guy."

"He already thinks it!" Bobby screams at the door.

"Then you have nothing to lose here, man!" I yell back.

"Fuck. Fuck, fuck, fuck, fuck!"

O'Dell and I lock eyes, and I shake my head. Bobby is spiraling and I thank Christ they ordered us to come get him. I couldn't handle him loose and fixated on Kyra in this state.

We hear what sounds like the shotgun being dropped to the floor. Half a second later, Dem confirms it.

O'Dell kicks the door open, barking orders to Bobby to lie down face first on the ground.

I'm right behind him, kicking the shotgun away and keeping my gun trained on him as O'Dell slaps a pair of metal cuffs on him.

Dem walks in ten seconds later, his gun drawn.

But I barely notice my partners because my gaze is tracing over the wall of driver's licenses hung like trophies and stuck on the collage of photographs of our sweet Kyra.

My voice shakes as I hiss, "Motherfucker."

ENTES TUERE
PUNIRE IMPIOS

Chapter Ten

O'DELL

I HAUL Bobby up by his biceps, prepared to walk him out of the building as quickly as possible, but my partners are gawking at the wall. I shove Bobby to his knees and tell him to stay still, only then allowing my focus to be pulled away from my criminal.

A chill shoots down my spine at over one hundred photographs of Kyra in various locations. Pictures that were taken as she walked through her apartment in the morning or down the street in the afternoon. Pictures of her training at her dojo, working her office job, or lastly, of her bartending at night.

"Motherfucker must've been following her for longer than she realized," Kerr growls, his gun still gripped in his hand.

"Watch your weapon," I say, swallowing down the bile rising in my throat.

Thoughts—dangerous ideas—run through my head. It would be so easy to kill Bobby right now. Take off the cuffs, put the gun back in his hands and shoot him in the head. No one would think twice and yet, for the first time in our lives, we have something to lose.

We finally have a shot at true happiness and creating a family with Kyra, and I don't want to throw it away on this bastard.

Dem pulls a picture of Kyra off the wall, inspecting it, memorizing every pixel. In it, she's just showered. Her hair's wet, and she's wearing a tank top and bikini panties. He's eerily quiet, his breathing ragged, as he stares at the photo.

Bobby makes the mistake of speaking out loud. "That's my girlfriend. Don't touch my pictures!"

I close my eyes for half a second, knowing Bobby has just signed his death certificate.

Dem spins around so quickly, I barely see him change his grip on his weapon, striking Bobby across the face with the butt of his gun.

Our rabbit goes down like a sack of potatoes, his body limp on the floor.

"We can't leave these here. If the Feds see these pictures, they're going to come looking for Kyra, which will open up a whole other can of fucking worms," Kerr looks at me.

"If we remove them and miss even one, they'll know we tampered with evidence, but worse, it could affect their case against the entire organization." My gaze purposely travels over to the wall of driver's licenses. There have to be at least fifty and in the three months we watched him, we saw him walk nearly twenty different girls through that house. Is this every girl that ever got abducted and sold by him? Do the other animals have similar trophy walls to this?

And why didn't DiFallo's goons torch this place earlier today when they came in? Maybe they never made it this far?

Can't ask Bobby. He's either out cold or dead.

"We have to leave it and we should get the fuck out of here before somebody else shows up looking for him."

Dem and Kerr both look down at the lump on the floor, their lips curled in disgust. I get their feelings—I really do—but I want to get this fucking nightmare over with and move on with our lives.

A life that includes Kyra.

I pull out my phone and take a couple of photos of the driver's licenses on the wall, texting them to our bureau contact.

> Me: Get a team down here before somebody from the family comes in and scrubs this place.

> Sandy: "Do you have Bobby Lash in custody?"

I kneel and check his pulse before I respond.

> "Yeah, but he's going to need medical attention."

Sandy: "Will take care of it when you get here. We have a collection team standing by. They can be there in a few minutes."

"How's the rest of the operation going?"

Sandy: "So far, so good. No shots were fired at any location. The other Townsend teams have secured their packages and are on their way in. You guys do good work."

"Yeah. We'll see you shortly."

I look at my partners, both of whom are shaking with rage. I fucking hate it when I have to be the calm and collected one of our team. However, this is why I am the lead, because I have a half an ounce more control over my temper than they do. That's how you get a bonus in your check, by being a bit less of a hothead.

"Let's get this shit bag handed over, turn in our gear, have a quick conversation with Townsend, and then go see our woman."

"If we leave these pictures, somebody's going to come looking for her," Kerr says again.

I nod. "She went through all the bullshit to get one guy sent to prison. If she has to, she'll do it again."

Dem shakes his head. "I don't like it."

I inhale deeply and exhale slowly, rolling my shoulders. "I don't like it either, but we can't tamper with evidence without possibly fucking over these other women in the process. Do you want to risk their justice? I know if we asked Kyra, she wouldn't."

Tying this back to Kyra and what she would want seems to snap them out of their rage-induced haze.

Kerr grumbles and holsters his weapon. "I'll get the truck."

Dem's eyes slide back to the lump on the floor. "Is he dead?"

"Despite your best effort? No."

He sneers and holsters his weapon. I stuff my phone in my pocket and help him lift Bobby's dead weight. We carry him out to the truck where Kerr has backed up to the apartment entrance with the backdoors wide open. We unceremoniously dump him in the back, slamming the doors shut.

The two guys with the pit bull edge closer, but seem smart enough to stay out of reach. "Hey man, is that Bobby?"

"What's it to you?" Dem arches his brow.

The guy without the dog throws his hands up and takes a step back. "The guy gave my girl the creeps. I figured if the cops came around, it'd be for him."

"Perfect timing," I mutter as the collection team arrives on scene. Pointing to three people I don't know, I tell the guy. "Tell them, if they ask. We've got to go."

We drive to the FBI building downtown, meeting Caiden, Case, and Porter in the underground garage.

Case arches his brow at the empty backseat. "Where's your rabbit?"

Kerr opens the backdoor to reveal Bobby, who started moaning two minutes ago. "In the trunk where the rabbit food belongs."

"Damn," Porter says. "He looks like expired hamburger meat. Did he fall down a flight of stairs?"

"Something like that," Dem shakes hands with Caiden.

"How'd your extractions go?" I ask.

"A lot better than yours, I'm thinking." Case shakes his head and turns away from Bobby, grimacing. Yeah, his face is purple, swollen, and bloody, and if he doesn't lose a tooth or two, I'll be surprised. Dem got him good.

"Where's Lee and Reese?"

"Inside with Victor and our handler, Sandy." Case points to the elevator. "Third floor, first door on the right. They're waiting for you. We'll show the guys where to take Bobby."

"Thanks." I shake Case's hand, pulling him in close. "Don't let my guys shoot him. They really want to."

Case chuckles. "I'll do my best."

There are two sections of every three-letter government building. The forward-facing one with marble floors, large windows, conference rooms, and brightly lit offices. You access those areas through the front door or guest garage. Then there are the tactical areas, the ones with no windows and dimly lit hallways. Those are the ones I always walk through, just like now.

Victor, Reese, and Lee are talking with Sandy around a table, my pictures highlighted on an oversized screen.

Both team leaders nod their heads as Sandy shakes my hand. "How's Bobby?"

"Breathing," I mutter and take the seat next to Lee.

"You don't sound very happy about that." Sandy, a

male with the last name of Sanderson, sits across from us. He points to the pictures on the screen. "We've already identified a handful of women from your photo. When our collection team gets done at his apartment, we'll have a gold mine of evidence."

"Did any of your rabbits have similar trophy walls?" I look to Reese and Lee, who both shake their heads.

"Not out in the open like yours."

"What's on your mind, O'Dell?" Victor sits forward.

Dammit. Normally, I wouldn't talk about this outside of our private walls, but I need Sandy's cooperation on this.

"There's a complication. Your team is currently collecting a wall of photos of one woman. A shrine, if you will," I lock eyes with Victor, letting him know exactly who I'm talking about. "I know the woman. I have a personal relationship with her and while Bobby was obsessed with her, she knows nothing about the human trafficking empire. He was stalking her and maybe it could have gone somewhere criminal, but then she met me."

Sandy narrows his eyes. "You're not trying to convince me that the guy you've had under surveillance for the last three months, the one who now needs medical attention, was coincidently stalking your girlfriend—are you?"

"During our surveillance, I noticed him watching her, which put her in my path. What I'm saying is this has nothing to do with the DiFallo human trafficking empire and considering she's been brutalized in the past, I would find it a professional courtesy to do everything in your power to keep her out of this."

He closes his eyes for a second and then locks gazes with Victor, who says nothing, even though the look on his face says everything. They don't want us as an enemy. We do the things they don't want traced back to their organization. Too many cameras and whistleblower websites exist nowadays, and even badass FBI agents have to be careful. But we don't exist when we don't want to and that's the beauty of being a private contractor.

"I'll do my best to separate the evidence. If I can, I'll lose it. But if we find we need to talk to her, I'll come to you to arrange the conversation."

"That's all I'm asking for."

"Why didn't you destroy the pictures?"

"Because I didn't want to risk contaminating any of the other evidence."

Sandy nods. "I appreciate that. You're sure she has no information about our case."

"One hundred percent."

He and I stare at each other for a hot minute. I know he has a dozen questions on the tip of his tongue, but I guess he respects me or values the relationship between the bureau and Townsend Agency, because he shakes his head and swallows them down. Then he slaps his thighs and stands, our silent invitation to leave. "Well, gentlemen. The bureau appreciates all you did here. I know this was a few-weeks-long assignment that dragged into months, and I appreciate your patience while we got our shit together."

He shakes each one of our hands, and the four of us head down to the garage together, saying nothing. In a three letter agency building, you never know who is listening.

Only when we are huddled between our trucks does Victor raise his brow and say in a low voice, "A shrine, huh?"

I nod and show him the pictures I didn't send to the Feds. "She was days away from a very bad situation."

"I guess she's lucky she blew up the house you were watching."

"We were all lucky."

"Well, it's over now," Victor slaps my shoulder. "You guys have some downtime. Go claim your woman."

Victor is fully aware of his teams' sexual and romantic predilections, as he himself was once the member of a team who also looked for that one special woman. Unfortunately, he lost one of his team members during a firefight—the last time he was in combat before he pinned on Colonel—and as far as I know, he's been single ever since.

Not that he doesn't know how to have a good time. We've seen him at The Access Club on more than one occasion.

"Gentlemen," Victor raises his voice a bit. "It's been a long three months, and I appreciate you doing the shit work assigned to us with little to no complaint. My business partner is coming to town, and I'm throwing a party at our favorite spot—next Saturday, six pm, VIP lounge."

"Until then, you are dismissed." Victor nods and then walks to his car, never tossing us a backward glance.

Caiden grins. "Our ladies obviously know each other, but do you have a date for the ball?"

I nod, but it's Kerr who answers. "We sure the fuck hope so."

"Cool. You guys have a week to make it happen. Until then..." Caiden salutes the group and walks with Reese and Soren to their vehicle. Lee, Case and Porter are already entering theirs.

I walk around to the driver's side door and pull my phone out of my pocket, checking our group text to realize I missed an entire conversation.

Kyra: I'm at the bar. No crazy stalkers seen on my way here.

Kerr: Bobby is secure. He will no longer bother you.

Dem: What time do you get off work?

Kyra: I'm closing tonight. So, one or two, depending on how busy we get.

Kerr: You want us to bring you dinner?

Kyra: You keep spoiling me like this and I'm going to expect it all the time.

Dem: You should expect it all the time. You have three men who want to worship and cherish you, so get used to being treated like a princess.

Kyra: I've never been a princess once in my whole life.

Kerr: That's because you're not a princess. You're a fucking queen. Specifically, our Queen.

Kyra: How soon can you guys get here?

Dem: We're waiting for O'Dell to finish briefing our boss, then we'll get ourselves cleaned up and be on our way. And we'll bring you dinner, but it's going to be a surprise.

Kyra: I'll eat anything you put in my mouth.

Kerr: Oh Kitten, we're going to keep your mouth very busy.

I'm glad the guys have been flirting with her for the last twenty minutes. It put them in a good mood, which means I will soon be in a good mood, too. As far as I'm concerned, she doesn't need to know what we found in Bobby's apartment—although, if she asks, we will tell her the truth. We'll never lie to her, even if we believe it's what is best.

"You guys ready to claim our queen?" I say as we pull out of the FBI parking lot, free for the first time in months.

"More than ready," Kerr says.

"Let's do it," Dem agrees.

Here we fucking go...

ENTES TUERE
PUNIRE IMPIOS

Chapter Eleven

KYRA

JIMMY THE BOUNCER is sitting at the bar tonight, his first night back after being jumped three weeks ago. The healing cuts and yellowish bruises on his face make my heart clench.

"Here you go, buddy." I slide a beer his way.

It's a Thursday night, so he's not scheduled to work, but I think he feels the need to protect me. He's never asked me out, nor indicated he was interested, and I'm afraid to ask if he has developed a crush. I don't think my three knights in shining armor would approve of a fourth suitor.

"You know," I lean forward so I can speak low, "you don't have to worry about me anymore. Bobby got locked up today. He won't be coming around again."

Jimmy arches his brow. "Are you sure?"

I slide my palm on his forearm and squeeze. "Yeah."

He lays his hand over mine. "Thank god. I was really worried about you."

A man clears his throat at the end of the bar. "Can we order a drink?"

I turn to find my men watching us, and they do not look happy. "Hi."

"Hey." O'Dell's eyes slide from me to Jimmy and back to me.

Smiling, I pat Jimmy's hand covering mine and pull away. "Guys, this is Jimmy. The bouncer I told you about."

Kerr walks a few feet down the bar and offers his hand. "Kyra told us what happened. How are you feeling?"

Poor Jimmy looks so confused. "Uh, I'm fine. Thanks for asking. Who are you?"

"We're Kyra's friends," Kerr says.

Dem follows and offers his hand. "Her close friends."

Jimmy's brow furrows even more. "Oh... kay."

"What can I get you guys to drink?" I interject, trying to pull their focus away from Jimmy. He's a big guy, but these three are just as big and ooze power and authority, the kind Jimmy at twenty-three years old hasn't mastered yet with all of his gym muscles. There's a big difference between his bulk and the three men honed from years of combat training.

Kerr locks eyes with me, his bright blue eyes shining in the darkness. "Come here, Kitten."

I know I shouldn't run to him, especially when he's making a blatant territorial claim on me—Jesus Christ, he might as well pee on me in front of Jimmy—but something about the look on his face says he needs this more than I do.

I round the end of the bar. "What's wrong?"

Kerr doesn't hesitate to pull me against his chiseled chest, cocooning me in his embrace. "I missed you."

I giggle, rubbing his back. "You saw me less than six hours ago."

"It feels like an eternity," Kerr pulls back and looks me in the eye. "If I paid you a month's worth of tips right now, would you blow off work and come home with us?"

"A whole month?" I joke.

"A year," he growls. "Name your price and I'll pay it."

I frame his face with my hands, barely remembering where we are or our audience. "I'd like nothing more than to come home with you right now, but Tony's short-staffed and has always been good to me. His wife just had their baby, and he's entrusted me with his bar while he's home taking care of them."

"If you come home with us, you won't have to work ever again if you don't want to."

I roll my eyes and smack his chest, taking a step back. "Yeah, right."

I turn into Dem's chest, having no idea he was waiting behind me. He wraps his arms around me, his hard body like pressing up against a hot stone.

"Hey there," I squeak in surprise.

He presses a kiss to my cheek, but then steps back, his eyes surreptitiously sliding toward Jimmy. Although he doesn't say a word, both of their actions speak loud and clear. I'm theirs and they will tolerate no one else making a claim. Considering my past, I should be terrified and yet, I'm not. If anything, I'm all warm and fuzzy inside because I know they'd never hurt me to get my undying loyalty. They want it freely and will worship and adore me to get it.

"We'll take a round of whiskey, Angel."

I smile, hoping to convey my understanding with the simple gesture. "Coming right up."

"Jimmy, do you drink whiskey?" Dem says.

"Uh, actually, I think I'll take off, but thanks anyway." Jimmy tosses a ten-dollar bill down on the bar. "See you tomorrow, Kyra."

"Keep your money, man. We'd be honored to buy you a drink."

He narrows his eyes. "Another time."

I watch this exchange, pouring them two fingers each of the best whiskey we have in the bar. After Jimmy leaves, I put the three glasses on a tray and walk out from behind the bar to serve them. "What the hell was that?"

"Nothing," Kerr grins. "We honestly wanted to buy the guy a drink. He put his pretty face in jeopardy to protect you."

I hand him a glass and sneer, "You can't be territorial over me like that."

"We told you we were possessive, Cupcake," O'Dell takes a glass from me.

"Jimmy's a nice kid." I hand Dem the last glass.

"A nice kid who should have taken his shot a while ago. He obviously wants to, but now it's too late." Dem takes it from me and winks.

I narrow my eyes and purse my lips. "If you guys are going to be jerks, I'm going home alone tonight." Yeah, I might like them claiming me, but I can't let them get away with this behavior—at least, not without checking them on it. I'm not some wallflower that will cower when they puff up in front of me.

I turn to walk away, but O'Dell grabs my arm, spinning me into his chest. "I haven't gotten my hug yet."

He pulls me into his arms, but unlike Kerr and Dem who kept their touches PG, O'Dell pulls me in between his splayed knees, wrapping one arm low across my back to pin me in place. He looks me in the eye while gently stroking my jaw with his free hand. "Don't be mad at us. We had a rough afternoon and you are the only balm to soothe our nerves. Besides, Jimmy is pretty."

"Shut up," I giggle, but then realize what he said. "Why was it rough? Are you hurt?"

His eyes light up. "I like that you're concerned about us. That is the first time we have had that. We need it. We need you."

I lean forward, pulled into his orbit. "I need you, too."

O'Dell presses his lips together, his thumb pulling my bottom lip down. "Fuck, I want to kiss you right now, but you have customers."

I look over at the bar and curse under my breath. "Shit."

For the next two hours, I schlep drinks and talk to my men when I have a break, taking bites of the dinner they ordered between customers.

It's after ten and the bar is fairly empty, which gives

me hope I can close early. Every time I walk past my men, one of them touches me, causing my pulse to race and my pussy to clench. Kerr keeps up the dirty talk, telling me how much he's looking forward to drizzling caramel sauce over my breasts and licking it off my nipples. He's already stolen a bottle from behind the bar.

Dem and O'Dell are getting a little bolder with their touches, pulling me in to kiss my neck, my chest—all while sliding their hands over my ass or between my legs.

They've all been nursing their whiskeys, so I know they're not drunk.

They're impatient, and my patience is wearing thin along with theirs. I can't wait to strip off our clothes and feel them touching every inch of my body. Sitting between Kerr and Dem this morning, touching both of them while they caressed and kissed me was so empowering—I can't wait to do it again.

Plus, I've been on edge all day, turned on and wanting more. I want to release. Soon.

I'm glad they came home safe and sound, because now, tonight, they can take me over the edge.

By eleven, the bar has been empty for thirty minutes. I text Tony and ask him if I can close early, to which he responds with '*have a good night.*'

To my surprise, as soon as I lock the front and back doors, my men help me clean up.

O'Dell points to a camera in the bar's corner—the one that looks over the cash register. "Are there any other cameras in here besides that one?"

"Not that I know of."

Kerr grins and pulls the glass out of my hand, setting it down on the bar. "So, you're saying there are no cameras overlooking this pool table right here?"

I frown. "No. Why?"

He lifts my fingers to his mouth, kissing each tip playfully, and walks me backwards until my ass hits the edge of the table. "Because I've waited long enough and I don't want to wait anymore."

Dem walks up beside us as the bar lights dim, the light over the pool table highlighting the altar on which they plan to lay me out.

Being a sacrifice never looked so tempting.

Kerr claims my lips, his hands cupping my ass and lifting until I'm sitting on the edge of the table. Tony would die if he knew I was sitting on his pool table, much less being laid out by three men as they undo the buttons of my jeans.

"Are you going to let me tongue fuck you, Kitten?"

"Now?" I gasp as he slips his fingers underneath the band of my bikinis, his thumb zeroing in on my clit like a metal detector.

His grin widens. "Right. Fucking. Now."

My zipper slides down—Dem is beside us, working my jeans down my legs while Kerr keeps me enthralled with his lips.

I'm definitely seeing the advantage of working together as a team.

"Lie back, Kitten. Let me taste you."

Before I can answer, Dem is kissing me, guiding me to my back, his tongue tangling with mine and taking away my ability to think. I slide my fingers into his hair, kissing him hard at the same time as Kerr slides my panties off my ass.

I gasp the moment Kerr slides his tongue up my pussy, his thumbs pushing back my labia so he can lap at my juices. "Fuck, Kitten, you are delicious."

Kerr is a master with his tongue, knowing exactly when to lick and when to suck and occasionally when to nibble. As my orgasm builds, my hips buck and Dem finally lets me catch my breath.

"Where's O'Dell?" I pant, remembering how they said he'd want to witness my climax.

"I'm right here, Cupcake," he pushes himself off the wall and emerges out of the darkness like a phantom.

"Oh god, yes. Yes. Right there, Kerr. Don't stop," I cheer Kerr on, but I'm looking at O'Dell, who stands by stoically with his hands shoved in his pockets while Dem fondles my breasts.

As if the only word Kerr heard was *stop*, he slows down and licks me gently.

"No. No, no, no—don't stop." Kerr responds by kissing my thigh.

"No! Dammit Kerr! Don't stop. I was so close."

Dem chuckles. "We know, Angel, but we want you to hold it for us until we get you home."

"Are you fucking kidding me?"

Dem shakes his head sadly, but the smile on his lips and sparkle in his eyes says he feels anything but remorse.

Fuck me! So, this is edging?

ENTES TUERE
PUNIRE IMPIOS

Chapter Twelve

DEM

KYRA IS PISSED as Kerr slides her panties up her legs. "You're not kidding?"

"No, Cupcake. We're not," O'Dell reaches out and caresses her cheek. "But we promise it will be worth it."

"But..." She reaches out and strokes O'Dell through his trousers.

"Mmmm," he growls and leans into her touch. "You can keep doing that, but it won't get you what you want."

She drops her hand and pushes Kerr back, jumping from the table. "I am not playing with you guys."

I grab her arm and spin her into my chest. "Angel, please. Trust us to take care of you."

"I did trust you and you failed."

Kerr chuckles and hands over her jeans. She snatches them from him while glaring at me. "This is torture."

"Pleasure torture—yes, it is. But once you come, you're going to fly so high, you might forget where you are for a minute."

I slide my hands around her waist, pulling her hips into mine, letting her feel how hard I am. "I'm aching too. We all are. Don't you think we're dying to feel you climax around our cocks?"

Kerr comes up behind her, pressing his cock into her ass. Her eyes grow wide as he grinds his hips. "We want you so fucking badly, Kitten. Let us play with you. It won't be much longer—I promise."

"You guys are assholes," she grumbles and glances between us.

O'Dell grins. "That sounds like a yes, boys."

Twenty minutes later, we're driving on the freeway. O'Dell's driving the truck and I have Kyra in the backseat with me. Kerr is following in her car.

Kyra is straddling my lap and grinding down on my cock, doing her best to tease me as badly as we have teased her. I know this game. It's a battle of wills. She thinks she can push me into taking her right now and giving her what she wants.

Don't get me wrong. I want to.

I want to feel my cock so deep inside of her and fuck her so hard that she gushes all over me.

And I will, but not until her clit is swollen and her g-spot spongy. I know it's frustrating to deny her—it's just as frustrating for us to deny ourselves. But it's also a lot of fucking fun.

"Don't you want to fuck me, Dem?" Kyra purrs in my ear.

"Very much so, Angel."

She reaches between our bodies, stroking my cock

through my slacks. "Now?"

"Not just yet."

She slumps on my lap. "This is bullshit."

O'Dell chuckles from the front seat.

Brushing back her hair, I hook my finger under her chin and lift her face. "There will be many times in the future when I will fuck you anytime, anywhere. Since tonight is your first night with the three of us, we need to share you."

She seems surprised. "So, after tonight, it could be me and you, or me and Kerr, or me and O'Dell?"

"Or any combination thereof," O'Dell adds.

"Absolutely," I nod. "I would never deny my brothers their opportunity to pleasure you, just like they'll never deny me. But we want to start this relationship right and the good thing about us... we're not greedy."

"We're a little greedy, but only in the absolute best way," he quips.

"I'm feeling greedy right now," Kyra says as she slides her hand back between us, her fingers moving in a counterclockwise motion against the hard bulge in my pants.

"And that is exactly the way we want you, Angel."

"We're home," O'Dell announces as he pulls through the gate onto our property.

We live in a high-end gated community on the outskirts of Chicago, which is extra nice considering none of us came from money. Between our military retirements, six-figure salaries and nearly fifteen years of solid investments, we live very well for three working-class stiffs who basically grew up on government subsidies.

Another benefit of our lifestyle—we pool our resources.

"Holy shit," Kyra hisses as she gets her first look at what we hope will be her new home.

"Our house is relatively modest for the neighborhood, but we think you'll like it."

"I am so embarrassed you guys had to eat lunch in my crap-hole of an apartment."

I turn her face back to me so I can look her in the eyes. "Don't ever be embarrassed about where you came from. Trust me, your apartment is luxurious compared to where Kerr grew up, and our childhood homes weren't much grander."

"There is one problem with our place, Cupcake," O'Dell parks in the garage and turns off the engine, turning around to face her. "It's severely lacking a woman's touch."

"Maybe you can help us with that."

Kerr swings the back door open and offers her his hand. "Come, Kitten."

She narrows her eyes, still pissed at him. "I was about to earlier."

He grins. "Keep being sassy and we'll see how long we can drag this out."

She slams her lips together and takes his hand.

Good girl. She learns quickly.

I follow behind them with O'Dell bringing up the rear.

"Do you want something to drink?" Kerr offers.

"Water," O'Dell answers for her.

She spins around and looks at him. If she's thinking about arguing, something on his face convinces her not to. "Water sounds great."

No alcohol tonight. Nothing to dampen the energy exchange between us. She needs to be one hundred percent connected to us until she passes out from sheer exhaustion, wrung dry from multiple intense orgasms.

That's the plan, anyway.

We walk through the living room to a corner bar with an ice machine that makes fancy cubes. We each have our vices, the one or two things from our childhood we dreamed of having if we were ever rich and powerful. Fancy, crunchy ice is Kerr's thing. So are the arcade games downstairs with a full-sized Tekken 3 and House of the Dead 2, as well as a couple of pinball machines. I'm sure he'll take her down there eventually, bend her over a pinball table and fuck her until they get a new high score.

My vice is the heated pool out back. I love to swim and was thinking about cross-training so I could become a Navy SEAL before PsySpecOps recruited me. And yes, I will definitely be cock-deep inside her in that pool one day.

Kerr hands her a glass of water.

She grins. "Crunchy ice?"

"We got a snow cone machine, too," he waggles his eyebrows.

"I love crunchy ice. It's my favorite thing about getting fountain soda at the corner market."

Kerr slides his hand into her hair and pulls her lips to his. "I fucking knew you were perfect."

I walk up behind her and slide my hand down the back of her jeans, gripping her belt loop and pulling her back from Kerr's hypnotizing mouth. "Let's go upstairs."

O'Dell takes the ice water out of her hand and gives it to Kerr, then he swings her up into his arms, carrying her up the stairs. This is a six-bedroom, eight-bath house with a game room and a weight room in the basement. Her bedroom has been sitting empty since we moved in. The only furnishing is a custom-made bed that is twenty-four inches wider than a California King. We knew we'd claim our woman someday, and she'd have the bed that could accommodate us all.

Otherwise, it's hers to furnish however she wants—not that she knows that yet. We'll spring that on her later.

"Can I ask a question that might be offensive?" Kyra asks from O'Dell's arms.

"You can ask us anything and everything, Angel. We have no secrets from you." I wink at her from behind his shoulder.

"Obviously, you guys have done this before."

"Is that the question?" Kerr chuckles, pulling off her shoes as we enter the bedroom and tossing them over his head.

"No, I'm trying to set expectations."

O'Dell sets her down on the bed and takes a step back. The three of us stare down at her, probably resembling a pack of horny, hungry dogs—without the snarling and foamy mouths.

"We won't do anything you don't want to do—" O'Dell starts.

"Besides edging," I cut in.

"Besides that, but deep down, you want it. Or at least you will once it's all over."

"I expect that you'll all be with me..." she hedges.

"Are you asking about anal, Kitten?" Kerr asks impatiently. Honestly, I'm surprised he's not already naked and stroking his massive cock in her face.

Her eyes grow wide. "No, although I guess I probably should be."

I sit down next to her on the bed and take her hand. "We have all the time in the world, Angel. At some point, someday, we'll want to take you together, which will mean double penetration, anal, all of it... but we're in no hurry. When you're ready, you'll tell us."

"And we'll be thrilled to answer your call," Kerr nods with a giant, goofy grin on his face that makes her roll her eyes.

"That's good to know, but that wasn't the question. I was wondering if you were intimate with each other?"

"Oh," I say, slightly surprised, even though I shouldn't be. Many women we've played with over the years have asked the same question.

"We're not bisexual," O'Dell states plainly.

"Although when we're with you, nothing stops us from pleasuring you. I've seen, smelled, and in some ways, felt everything my brothers have to give. It doesn't bother us, but we don't seek pleasure from each other,"

Kerr adds. "Let me guess, you didn't even know this was a thing outside of porn?"

She blushes. "Yeah."

"So, you watch porn?" His smile gets so big, I think his face is going to crack.

Kyra narrows her eyes. "I'm going to give you another black eye."

"We have a sparring ring downstairs. Anytime you want to wrestle, I'm your guy."

"Do you have any other questions, Cupcake?" O'Dell rolls his eyes at Kerr.

She looks from Kerr to O'Dell and then to me. "Are you still hard from earlier?"

O'Dell and I both grab one of her hands and press it against our cocks.

"Yes," we say in unison.

Her face lights up. "How do we begin?"

To answer her, I lean forward and capture her lips, slipping my tongue inside her hot, wet mouth. I hear Kerr and O'Dell unbuttoning their shirts and kicking off their shoes while I slide my hands under her shirt, pulling it over her head. Standing, I pull her into my arms, continuing to kiss her as Kerr walks up behind her, his hands circling her waist and going to the buttons on her jeans. He's kissing her shoulders and drops low to pull her jeans down her long legs.

"Ow!" She jumps, and I'm betting Kerr bit her ass, considering he's chuckling.

I unfasten her bra and then take a step back, getting my first look at our woman completely naked. She's beautiful, but bruised, and I know I'm not the only one bothered by it when O'Dell curses under his breath.

Gently, I caress her skin. "Are these all from yesterday?"

She looks down and nods. "Yeah, but they're not much worse than the ones I get sparring at the dojo."

"I didn't notice them under the dim lights on the pool table."

Kyra cradles my face in her hands. "Don't go getting all soft on me now. I'm not suddenly a delicate flower. I'm still the woman who almost kicked Kerr's ass yesterday, remember?"

Speaking of the devil. He scoops her up and drops her on the bed, plopping down beside her and caressing her breasts with his fingertips. "Yeah, Dem. She's fine. She's with us. I've already told you she's delicious. Now, are you going to take a taste or not?"

The look he flashes to O'Dell and I says, *Snap out of it and get into the moment. She doesn't want a bunch of sappy ass overprotective bullshit from us. She wants men who will cheer her on as she kicks ass, handing her whatever weapon she wants to wield.*

Silently, I nod, remembering what plans we have for our woman.

I work the buttons on my shirt as O'Dell climbs onto the bed. Both my partners are naked and spread out next to her, O'Dell kneading her breasts and sucking on her nipples as Kerr kisses her breathlessly, his fingers sliding between her legs.

He growls, "You're so wet. Are you going to ride Dem's tongue like you did mine?"

I slide off my pants and then crawl on the bed between her legs, sliding my hands up the outsides of her thighs and looking down at her, waiting for her to answer.

Her eyes sparkle as she looks up at me. "Yes."

Smiling, I lift her leg in the air, kissing her calf before resting it on my shoulder. "Remember what I told you, Angel. To the edge, over and over again, until you beg."

I lower my head and run my tongue over her slick folds, murmuring my agreement with Kerr. "Absolutely delicious."

Then I bury my face in her pussy, working her clit hard and fast. I suck her engorged pearl against my teeth, her hips jerking against my mouth as she moans. It takes a few minutes before she's bucking against my tongue like she did with Kerr, her heels digging into my shoulder blades as she says, "Yes. Right there. Please."

I slow down, flicking her clit gently and then flattening my tongue to lick her like an ice-cream cone. I alternate between the two, occasionally blowing air against her plump clit to keep her aroused.

"Please," she whimpers as her orgasm ebbs.

"Not yet, Kitten," Kerr growls as she grips his cock in her hand.

Pushing her legs up, I re-attack, licking and sucking until she's writhing underneath me again. As soon as I think she's close to coming, I stop and look up between her legs to survey the scene. She's got both Kerr and O'Dell by their cocks, stroking as Kerr feeds her his fingers—but what he needs to be doing is feeding her his cock. Keeping her mouth busy will engage her mind, giving me more latitude to work her body into a frenzy.

I trail kisses up her stomach and to her chin.

She's panting, the gleam in her eye promising me retribution.

"How good are you at giving head, Angel?"

Sucking on an ice cube that Kerr has fed her, she clears her throat. "I'm great at it. Why? You want to let me tease you for a while?"

I grin. "No. I want you to tease one of them while I go back to eating your pussy."

I exchange a look with Kerr and O'Dell to say *get a dick in her mouth so I can play.*

Kerr motions to O'Dell to take the lead.

The mattress shifts as O'Dell gets up on his knees and moves above her head while I kiss her soft belly and settle back between her legs, sucking her clit into my hungry mouth.

Now it's time to really play.

ENTES TUERE
PUNIRE IMPIOS

Chapter Thirteen

O'DELL

DEM IS RIGHT. We're treating Kyra with kid gloves, which isn't like us at all. But the last thing I want to do is scare her. I know we would never hurt her on purpose, but she's got a bunch of shit to unpack and honestly, we should focus solely on her pleasure and comfort.

"Hey, Cupcake," I smile down at her with my hard erection throbbing in my hand.

"I was wondering when one of you was going to feed me the beast between your legs."

"We didn't want to rush you."

"Think you could choke me with him?" She lifts her eyebrows in challenge and all my concerns melt away.

Goddamn, she's fucking perfect for us. Strong, smart, and sarcastic. Her quick tongue will keep us on our toes for a lifetime.

"Do you think you can take all of him?" I challenge her back.

"I'm willing to try," she opens her mouth and sticks out her tongue, swiping at the bead of pre-cum threatening to drip from the head of my cock.

I growl, the feel of her tongue too good to fight the urge building in my balls. Slowly, I feed her my length until I see the outline in her throat and then I pull back at the sound of her gagging.

"Mmmm. More," she wraps her fingers around the base and feeds herself, taking control from underneath.

I close my eyes, letting the feel of her mouth permeate my soul. She works me slow and soft, then fast and hard, in time with Dem's ministrations and her building orgasm. When I open my eyes, Kerr has his head resting on her sternum as he plucks and plays with her nipples, smiling up at me.

"What the fuck are you smiling at?" I hiss.

"She's a talented girl," he responds, like it's obvious.

"Yeah, she is. Maybe you should feel her for yourself?"

Kyra pants hard, my cock falling from her lips. "Yes. Oh god, Dem. Please don't stop."

She moves to grab Dem's head to hold him in place, but Kerr and I pin her hands down. Kerr kisses her neck and nibbles on her ear to distract her as I fall back on my heels, continuing to stroke my cock.

Dem comes up from between her legs, grinning like a loon. He loves doing this shit and while I agree the denied orgasms equal a euphoric high later, continued denial can be extremely frustrating. "Okay, Angel. No more teasing. You ready to come for us?"

Kyra lifts up on her elbows, looking absolutely wrung out. "You promise?"

He slides two fingers inside her slowly. "Oh, yeah. You're more than ready. But the question is, how do we want to make you come?"

"Quickly, I hope!" she snaps.

We chuckle. "Doesn't work that way, Cupcake. Besides, I haven't had a taste of you yet."

Dem stands up on the edge of the bed and pulls her to her feet, cradling her against his chest. I prefer to eat pussy with her straddling my head and my partners know this. I lay down while Dem guides her over to the side of the bed.

"You want me to sit on your face?" Kyra gasps.

"Very much so." I lick my lips.

"I'll suffocate you." She giggles.

"What a way to go," I grab her hips and, with Dem's help, position her over my mouth. One swipe of my tongue and I groan, her pussy tasting like a candied apple, both sweet and tart at the same time. She's obviously worked up—her musky scent tells me that much—and I know it won't take a lot to send her over the edge. Between Kerr and Dem, they've driven her to the brink over and over again, but I'm the one to get the reward.

I fuck her cunt with my tongue, then flatten it out, running it over her asshole. Her thighs tighten around my head when I do, letting me know we'll have to train her for anal. I doubt she's done it before, but I'm hoping she'll want to with us. I'd love to be the one to pop that cherry for her.

Circling her asshole again, I move my mouth and use the scruff of two days' worth of growth to rub against her clit, her body vibrating above me.

"Lean back, grab your ankles, and point your chin to the ceiling," I growl as I dig my fingers into her ass cheeks and spread them, once again lapping at her ass until she relaxes into me. Then, she finally rides my tongue, chasing her release, and I egg her on, pushing and pulling her hips and latching on to her clit.

One suck against my teeth and she screams her release, gushing her arousal down my chin.

I suck her juices down and then roll her to her back, knowing my partners will want a taste of her, too. Kerr is sitting next to her head, smiling down at her as he swipes his finger along her quivering pussy and brings it to his lips. "Delicious, right?"

"Warm and comforting, like apple pie," I wipe my face and sit up, watching her ride orgasmic waves of pleasure.

Dem sits a little further down and rubs her legs, waiting for her to come back to us. "She's going to become addicted to us, to this, and we'll take perfect care of her, always."

Every orgasm denial is different—just like every woman, every night, and every experience. We've seen women float off into subspace after hours of hard play and extensive denial, and then we've seen women speak in tongues—cursing everyone but their grandmother— only to come back to themselves with little recollection of the filthy things that came out of their mouth.

Kyra rides the waves in relative silence, touching herself lightly like a Catholic schoolgirl on ecstasy, exploring herself for the first time. It's intoxicating to watch and, like Dem said, addicting to experience.

She opens her eyes slowly, like she's waking from the best dream, and smiles up at us. "Hey."

"How do you feel?"

She throws her head back and stretches like a kitten, which makes Kerr grin. "You were right. That was amazing."

Kerr caresses the top half of her body with light strokes while Dem handles the lower half, leaving me to contemplate what is next.

Kyra reaches over and rubs my thigh, walking her fingers toward my cock. I know she's fully back to herself when she smiles and says, "Who's going to fuck me first?"

I glanced at Dem, who shakes his head. He's right, this encounter has been a lot more awkward than normal. Is that because Kyra is special to us and not just a mutually beneficial good time? Is it because of the way we met —exploding house, psycho stalker, and human trafficking empire? Or is it because of her past trauma and our fear of triggering her?

Perhaps a combination of all three.

"Maybe I should get down on my knees and the three of you can surround me in a circle?"

Kerr laughs and climbs off the bed, grabbing his slacks and sliding them on.

I sigh and take her hand, pulling her into my lap. "Come here, Cupcake."

She nestles in my lap, but is looking at Kerr. "Why are you getting dressed?"

"You really have watched a lot of porn, but we aren't the circle jerk kind of guys." He walks over and caresses her cheek, flashing her a teasing smile.

She bites her lip and looks down. "I met Penelope Penshaw at the trial. The DA introduced us and I started attending her classes. They are so therapeutic, not just from the perspective of learning how to fight and protect myself, but by being immersed in a group of women who were also sad and angry and healing. This one woman had a similar brutal story to mine, but she was dating. She was in a healthy relationship. So, I asked her how she overcame her negative feelings about sex, because prior to being raped, I thought I had a fairly healthy sex drive. I wasn't falling into bed with every guy I met, but if I was attracted to him and I thought we'd have a good time, I didn't shy away from sex. I feel like it is part of a healthy relationship, you know?"

"Anyway, she's the one that turned me onto porn. She said in some ways it helps desensitize her and that the images of her attack were somehow muted. Not that she forgot, or forgave, but in her mind, she could compartmentalize what had happened to her away from new relationships. She told me I should focus on the aspects of sex I found pleasing, fantasize about those, and when I'm ready to date, I'd have the drive to make all my fantasies a reality."

"I can't change what happened that weekend. It happened, and it is what it is. But I didn't want him to take away the rest of my life in the process. That was his goal—to strip me of everything and break me—and I couldn't give him that."

"So yeah, I watch porn," she brings her eyes up at Kerr, a defiant spark in her blue orbs.

He drops to a knee beside us. "I'm not shaming you, Kitten. I understand getting into a relationship with three men is taboo and if one of your fantasies is to make a home video, I'm sure one day we can do that, but this is not porn. This is our lives we're offering you."

"I don't understand what that means."

I slide my hand into the back of her hair, playing with the strands, pulling her attention to me. "It means this isn't about sex. It's about becoming a family. It's about learning how you like your morning coffee and what side of the bed you sleep on and how angry you get when you're hungry."

"It's about knowing what movies make you cry and learning what your favorite foods are and figuring out new ways to spoil you," Dem adds as he rubs her back.

"And it's about sex," Kerr grins and waggles his brow.

I side-eye him and mutter under my breath, "Dick."

He laughs. "Come on, she expects that from me."

Kyra nods. "I totally do."

"We are very decisive men and rarely second-guess our decisions. It took no time for us to know you were special and that we want to build something with you. I understand this might be overwhelming, but we wouldn't have brought you here if we weren't already committed to you and us."

"This isn't the playroom you bring all your women to?"

I shake my head. "There's never been another woman on this bed or in this house. This room is yours when you decide you want it. We'll furnish it however you like, buy you whatever you want, and give you whatever you need."

Kyra glances from me, to Kerr, and then to Dem. "You're serious. This is mine?"

"Yes."

"And when you told me earlier tonight that if I came home with you, I would never have to work again?" She looks at Kerr.

"I meant every single syllable."

"Not that you have to quit your jobs in order to be with us, but the option is there," I say.

"Or you could go back to school," Kerr adds.

"Or do whatever you want," Dem finishes.

Kyra looks around the room, almost wistfully, taking in everything we've said. We sit by patiently, knowing this is a lot from one man, much less three. "I think I want to take a shower."

"Your bathroom is this way." Kerr offers his hand and leads her away from Dem and me.

"Why are we being so fucking awkward?" Dem says in a low voice.

"Uncharted territory. We actually care about her and the outcome of tonight," I say plainly. "This is a lot for all of us."

Dem rolls off the bed and grabs his clothes off the floor. "I'm going to clean up."

I nod and also stand. "Good idea."

ENTES TUERE
PUNIRE IMPIOS

Chapter Fourteen

"THIS IS MY BATHROOM?" I walk into the en suite, which is larger than my entire apartment. There's a huge glass-enclosed shower that could fit three, if not all four of us. And a big jacuzzi soaker tub that would be fun for at least two of us.

"We told the contractor to build every woman's fantasy bathroom."

"This would be it," I grin, my attention focused on a box on the counter. "What's in here?"

"Uh… that's not for right now," Kerr tries to stop me from opening the lid to find a variety of brand new sex toys still in the packaging.

"Are these for me?"

"They are for us. I've been collecting them for a while now," he shrugs.

"Before you met me?" I pull out a set of training plugs.

He grins. "I knew you were out there waiting for us, but we couldn't find you."

"Who would get the biggest kick out of me wearing one of these?" I crack open the packaging, running my fingers over the smooth silicone plug.

"It would get all of us going, but I think O'Dell would be the most affected."

"So, that's his thing? Anal."

Kerr shrugs, grabbing me a towel and a plush terrycloth robe and setting them on the counter. "Our thing, Kitten, is you," he turns the shower spray on, testing it, and then ushering me in.

"Aren't you going to take a shower with me?"

He frames my face and kisses my forehead. "Not tonight. I'm thinking the three of us at once might be a bit much for our first night, so I want you to take a hot shower and come find us when you're done. Let's relax, get to know each other, and not overthink this. Okay?"

"Okay," I watch him walk away as I step under the strong, hot spray. The shower is luxurious. The bathroom —my bathroom and adjoining bedroom—is more than I ever dreamed of having. They're offering it all to me, but why?

I have to admit that they make me feel something I haven't felt in a long time.

Seen? Very much so. They see me for who I am, scars and all.

Safe? Absolutely. Safer than I thought possible.

Desired? More than I've ever felt in my life.

Loved?

I tilt my head back and let the hot water pour over my face, realization hitting me square in the gut. They make me feel loved, and that scares the shit out of me. My parents weren't there for me growing up. I was a teenage mistake that never should have been, and was taking care of myself from the age of eight on. Although I always had a roof over my head and ramen in the pantry, I spent most of my life alone. My parents never married, although they did have an on-again-off-again relationship for the first ten years of my life. It was like one of them was always chasing the other, and then when they caught them, they were no longer interested. I have no foundation, no healthy example of what a loving relationship looks like, and because of that, I've never allowed myself to get close to a guy. I'm the queen of pushing them away before they can become attached.

Yet, these guys—these strong, dominant, alpha types—fell for me before I knew what was going on.

And dammit, I've fallen for them, too.

How the hell did this happen to me?

With my heart in my throat, I lather up my body, my clit still swollen and sensitive as I slide over it. Dem worked me good and I have to admit, my climax was unlike anything I've ever experienced.

Pleasure torture... who even knew such a thing existed?

I can't be afraid of the love they are so willing to give. I couldn't care less about taboo relationships. What friends do I have to worry about what they think, anyway? So, the only person who can fuck this up is me, and I refuse to do that.

I turn off the water, towel dry my hair, and don my new robe, intent on finding my men and making them mine. Digging through the sex box, I take out the smallest plug and a tiny packet of lube and slip them into my robe pocket.

As I round the corner into the kitchen, I hear O'Dell say, "The Access Club will be too much for her right now. Maybe in a few months, but next Saturday is too soon."

"What's The Access Club?" I ask, walking right into Dem's chest and wrapping my arms around him.

"Good shower, Angel?" He kisses my cheek.

"Fantastic. I think I'm going to like living here." I throw the statement out boldly, knowing I've hit my mark by the look the guys exchange. "So? The Access Club?"

O'Dell leans back against the counter and crosses his arms over his enormous chest. I haven't had a chance to appreciate their bodies yet, considering they've mostly had me on my back since we've been here. "It's a sex club downtown, Cupcake."

"Members only?" I guess.

"Yes."

"And how does one become a member?" I trace my fingers over Dem's flat, bare stomach, toying with the waistband of his pajama bottoms. His breathing changes slightly, but I pretend not to notice.

"You get sponsored. Our boss—well, it's one perk of our job." O'Dell's eyes follow my hands.

"Your boss? Why would he sponsor you at a sex club?"

Kerr is also watching me. He turns and grabs a spoon from the drawer and then pulls a pint of ice cream out of the freezer. "Our jobs can be stressful, and Victor wants to make sure we have a way to blow off steam."

"This is where you've played with other women and why none of them have been here?"

"Yes," Dem hisses as I slide my hand over his erection.

"Does your boss know about the three of you?"

"We're not the only ones," O'Dell says as an answer. "It's common in our world."

I slide my hand into Dem's pajama bottoms, gripping him tightly as I rub my thumb in tiny circles over the head, using his pre-cum to lubricate my finger. To keep the conversation going, I talk casually, even though my blood is pumping and my clit throbs. "What's going on next Saturday?"

"There's a private party. All the teams will be there," O'Dell's breathing sounds a bit labored, too.

"They will bring their women with them," Kerr sucks on a spoonful of ice cream, reminding me of the caramel sauce he stole from the bar. Maybe I'll ask him to make me a sundae later.

"To have sex?" My voice pitches in surprise.

"No," Dem shakes his head at the same time he arches into my hand. "We would never share you and they would never share their women. They'd gut us for even hinting at it."

"These are the families you mentioned before?"

"Yes." O'Dell's cock is hard in his loose pants. So is Kerr's.

"I want to go to a party." Pressing my lips together to suppress the giggle ready to erupt from my mouth at the look on all of their faces. I pull my hand out of Dem's pants and interlace our fingers, leading him back into the living room, hoping O'Dell and Kerr follow.

"Sit down, Dem." I drop to my knees in front of him, pulling the drawstring on his pants and releasing his cock for my viewing pleasure. Sliding my hand down his impressive length, I lick him from base to tip. "I haven't had a chance to appreciate you yet."

"You can do anything you want to me, Angel."

"Including teasing you mercilessly?"

"Especially that."

I swirl my tongue around the head and then take him as deep as I can. Dem groans, arching his hips and letting his head fall back. I brace myself on my elbows, pushing my ass in the air. Looking to my right, I find O'Dell standing on the threshold, leaning against the wall with his arms crossed over his chest, his cock straining against the flannel fabric of his pajama pants as he watches us. I reach into my robe pocket and show him what I have. "Would you help with this?"

He groans audibly and pushes himself off the wall, taking the silicon plug and lube from me. "Yes, I will."

Then he moves an ottoman over and playfully smacks my ass. "Kneel on this while you work Dem's cock."

I step up and resume my position, finding this a lot more comfortable. With my ass in the air, I can lean forward and take Dem's cock deeper in my mouth without contorting him at a weird angle. He seems to like it, too, as he threads his fingers in my hair to encourage me to take him harder, faster.

O'Dell steps behind me and flips my robe up over my waist, the cool air tickling my wet and tingly pussy. He slides his fingers over my lower lips, growling from behind me. "So fucking pretty."

A couple cool drops of lube drip down the crack of my ass, which he works over my asshole with a press of his thumb. The feeling is foreign and yet hot. So fucking hot. I spread my knees as far as the ottoman will allow me, continuing to work Dem's cock with loud, wet suction, moaning as O'Dell adds a little pressure and more lube. His thumb presses against the tiny rosette until he pushes past the muscle a fraction of an inch, causing my entire body to tense up.

"Shhhh, Cupcake." His breath is against my ass cheek. "Relax. I won't hurt you." With his thumb in my ass, he rotates his hand, sliding two fingers inside my pussy.

"Ah!" Dem's cock falls from my lips as I toss my head back.

He kisses me hard. "Your mouth is pure heaven, Angel."

"And your cock is amazing," I moan again as O'Dell rubs his thumb and fingers together inside of me.

"Does that feel good?" Kerr stands behind Dem, staring down at me.

"Yes," I gasp as O'Dell pushes his thumb in deeper, more lube being worked in and out of me.

"It's going to feel so good with that plug in your ass, Kitten. You're going to love it."

"Come here." I pat the cushion next to Dem before wrapping my lips around his beautiful cock again.

Kerr sheds his pants—not shy in the least—and sits hip to hip with Dem, who drops one of his hands from my hair. Somehow, my men shift underneath me, giving me access to both of them without losing O'Dell behind me. Kerr props his leg up between my splayed knees on the ottoman, giving Dem the idea to do the same. Then he's sliding his hand into my hair and pulling me off Dem's cock so he can kiss me hard.

O'Dell removes his fingers, sliding the plug up and down, teasing me with it. "Are you ready, Cupcake?"

I nod as Kerr releases me.

Dem leans forward, sliding his fingers down my belly to my clit while whispering in my ear. "Relax, Angel."

There's pressure and then a sense of fullness. I suck in my breath—my senses overloaded as Dem taps the pad of his finger against my clit.

"You okay?" Kerr grins, stroking himself in invitation.

"It feels weird," I moan, my eyes rolling back as Dem circles my clit harder.

"You'll get used to it," Kerr leans forward to whisper in my ear. "But you know what will feel amazing?"

"What?"

"Having O'Dell fuck you from behind with the plug in your ass."

ENTES TUERE
PUNIRE IMPIOS

Chapter Fifteen

KERR

I'M A PUPPET MASTER.

I always have been.

And I get off on it.

I'm the good idea fairy, floating around and filling people's heads with naughty ideas. Since I was a kid, I could read people, figure out their triggers and motivations, and then play upon them. That's why I'm always the one to meet the women we've played with, because I can suss out who is adventurous and who isn't—who wants a night of fun or a lifetime of commitment. I'm not an asshole. I never convince people to do something they don't want to do, but I encourage people to let go of their inhibitions and do the things gnawing at their insides.

I set beasts free—usually for pleasure, sometimes for punishment.

My talents aren't always used for good.

Kyra has worked hard to not be shackled by her past and I find her inspiring because of it. We can give her everything she needs and everything I think she's ready to receive.

She's drunk with pleasure as I pull back. "Feed me, Kerr."

I offer her my cock, bouncing the tip against her lips before sliding deep into her mouth. Dem is right, her mouth is pure heaven. She's perfect and sucks me hard with lots of saliva. Her mouth feels so good that I can't help but grab her head and fuck her pretty little mouth—wanting nothing more than to come down her throat. She quickly has me singularly focused, the urge to release taking over my thoughts, when I remember my brothers and my puppeteer duties.

I pull her off me and kiss her hard again. "Ask him, Kitten."

Kyra's panting. "Please fuck me."

I look up to make eye contact with him. He arches his brow in question.

"Ask him again, Kitten," I whisper in her ear while smirking at him.

Kyra looks over her shoulder. "Please fuck me, O'Dell. Now."

Don't have to ask him twice. He shoves his pajama bottoms down and grips his cock, sliding the tip up and down her pussy. When he slides forward, Kyra's mouth falls open, her eyes rolling back in her head.

"How do you want it, Kitten? Hard and fast? Slow and gentle? A bit of both?" I tease her earlobe between my teeth.

"Both," she gasps.

"You heard her." I nod at O'Dell at the same time as I lower her mouth back to my cock.

"Fuck," he growls from behind her, throwing his head back as he grips her hips. I watch it all—a ringmaster admiring his circus—clocking every movement as she strokes Dem while swallowing me and taking O'Dell deep with a plug in her ass.

Fuck, I couldn't be prouder of her right now.

"Good Kitten," I grunt. "I wish you could see yourself, taking care of your men at the same time."

"So fucking sexy," Dem agrees.

"Oh my god, she's so hot and tight," O'Dell groans.

I pull her off my cock, kiss her, and then guide her back to Dem.

O'Dell clenches his jaw, his hips moving faster with each pump of his hips.

Wrapping her fingers around my cock, I lean back and marvel at the feel of her.

This is our woman.

Ours.

Now and forever.

Tonight is only the beginning of our family, and the idea has me on the verge of exploding.

"Cupcake?" O'Dell growls. "Kyra, are you on birth control?"

She mewls, coming up for air long enough to say "Yes," before switching back to me to swallow my dick.

"I'm going to come," O'Dell grits out seconds before he lets loose, his fingers digging into her hips as he thrusts forward.

I slide my fingers into her hair, thrusting my hips up, also on the edge. I could come now, or I could not, but the primal predator in me wants to paint her with my cum, too. "Are you okay swallowing me, Kitten?"

She nods, tears falling from her eyes. I swipe them away with my thumb as I continue to fuck her mouth, chasing my orgasm. A few more pumps of my hips and I'm roaring my release, shooting my load down her throat. I hold her head against me as I pant for breath, aftershocks causing shivers to climb up my spine.

Finally, I slump back, falling from her lips. To our woman's credit, she barely spills a drop.

I bend down and kiss her hard again. "You okay?"

"Yes," she's also panting, her breath catching as O'Dell pulls out of her.

"Good," I chuckle, "because now I want you to crawl onto Dem's cock and fuck the ever-loving hell out of him."

She grins, her eyes sliding Dem's way with a mischievous glint to them. Fuck me, I think I found my partner in crime. The guys will never be safe from us.

He responds by wrapping his long fingers around her ribcage and pulling her into his lap.

I kick the ottoman out of the way so he can put his feet on the ground, lean back, tilt his hips up and slide inside of her.

Standing behind her, I cup and knead her breasts, plucking at her nipples, pulling her back flush against me as Dem grips her hips and moves himself slowly in and out of her.

She moans and lays her head back, her eyes on me. "So good."

"You like being fucked by your men, Kitten?"

"Yes."

I slide my hand up her throat, holding her in place with gentle fingers but a firm hand, feeling the need to confess my darkest secrets to her. "We're going to take care of you, Kyra. We're going to pleasure and play with you, provide for and protect you, cuddle and love on you —forever."

She licks her lips. "I love you, too."

ENTES TUERE
PUNIRE IMPIOS

Chapter Sixteen

HEARING her confession causes my rib cage to tighten and my heart to clench.

She's ours.

She's really ours.

Kerr locks eyes with me, expressing the same thoughts, and then kisses her sweetly before letting go.

I immediately pull her to my chest and claim her lips, fusing everything I'm feeling into this one kiss.

She leans her forehead against mine, sliding up and down slowly on my cock. "You guys certainly know how to show a girl a good time."

I chuckle. "You're not mad at me for teasing you?"

She shakes her head. "No. You were right. Even though it was pure torture, it was worth it."

She rolls her hips, making me groan. "Christ, you feel so fucking good."

"How do you like it, Dem? Slow and sensual?" She bounces hard once on top of me. "Hard and fast?"

"Mmmm. I like being inside of you," I look down at where we are joined, my cock sliding in and out of her perfectly.

"That's not an answer."

I look her in the eyes, her stormy blue orbs mesmerizing and beautiful. "But it's the truth, Angel. As long as I'm touching you, tasting you, pleasing you, providing for and protecting you, I'm a happy man."

She trails kisses along my jaw and sucks my earlobe in between her teeth, rolling her hips in slow, languid waves. "What if I went really slow? Would that drive you crazy?"

Chuckling, I grip her hips. "Are you teasing me?"

"Would that be wrong?"

"No. I like prolonging the release. I enjoy feeling it build in my balls. Tightening up as cum climbs to the tip on the verge of shooting out, only to back it down and start all over again. But you know what the best part is?"

"What?"

"I can fuck you for hours before I come."

Her jaw drops. "I don't think I can go that long."

"Not tonight, but someday."

She juts her bottom lip. "I don't think I want to go that long."

I wrap my arms around her and roll so she's underneath me on the couch. "Are you saying you want me to fuck you hard and fast?"

"I'm saying I want to come again, and this time I want you to come with me."

Pulling her leg up, I slide deep inside her, my thumb circling her clit. "Is that what you want?"

She moans, "Yes."

"Tell me." I quicken my thrusts as her cunt tightens around me. Her clit is so plump, so sensitive, that she reacts perfectly to my touch. It's heady and empowering to have her so responsive. "Tell me how badly you want to come."

"Please, Dem. Please make love to me and make me come."

Make love to me. If there was anything she could say to bring me right to the edge, that was it. "Oh Angel, you're perfect."

I pump my hips until she's chanting a series of *Oh gods* and *Yes, Yes, Yes,* my own orgasm begging to be set free.

"Fuck!" she screams, arching her back at the same time her cunt clamps down on me like a vice grip.

I growl and bury my face into her neck as I come, shooting long, thick ropes of cum up inside her. My entire body convulses, spurt after spurt rocketing out of me. One thing about me, when I do come, I come hard and shoot huge loads. Some women like it; some don't.

Kerr jokes it's because I cause too much to build up over time.

Whatever. It feels fucking amazing.

Speaking of the asshat. He rests his hip against the back of the couch, waiting for me to finish. "Ewww. Now we have to get the couch cleaned."

"Fuck you, Kerrigan," I growl, pulling my head up to look Kyra in the eye.

"He shoots the biggest loads, Kitten," he chuckles and throws a hand towel on my head, taking a step back before I swing at him.

"Kerrigan? Is that what Kerr is short for?" Kyra asks as I slide the towel underneath her, because even though he's an asshole, he's not wrong.

"Yeah, and Dem is short for Demitrius."

I pull out of her and sit back on my heels, watching my cum slide out of her soaked pussy with a sense of pride.

Mine. I mean, ours, but also definitely mine.

Kerr takes a step back. "That's a sexy sight."

"You like watching your cum slide out of me?" Kyra giggles, putting her arms behind her head, thrusting her breasts into the air. Seeing her laid out like that only causes my cock to stir again.

Kerr growls beside me, so I know he's thinking the same thing. "We like seeing our cum mark you, painting you from the inside out. It's stupid, animalistic and territorial, but it gets us hard nonetheless."

"Oh, fuck me. Good job, man," O'Dell walks up from behind me, getting a glimpse of my—technically our—handiwork.

"I'm feeling like a Picasso right now, guys. You're evaluating, scoring, and appraising my value for investment purposes," she giggles. The fact that she's not weirded out by us right now only emphasizes how perfect she is for us.

"You laid out like this is what I'd call a priceless work of art." I pull her leg up and kiss her inner thigh.

"Agreed." Kerr leans over the couch and sucks her nipple into his mouth. "If you're amenable, we can leave you here to lounge around all the time. Naked, of course."

She rolls her eyes. "Of course."

O'Dell hands her a mug. "Tea."

Kyra sits up, seemingly unashamed of her nakedness like the three of us. That's good, because something tells me we'll be happiest when she's naked. "Thank you."

"Do you want something to eat?"

She smiles up at Kerr. "I was thinking about that caramel sauce."

He grins. "That's going to get us very sticky."

"Well, you said you had to clean the couch, anyway," she giggles. "I'm kidding. I'm thinking about taking another shower and then maybe, bed."

I nod. "It has been a crazy couple of days. It would be nice to get a good night's sleep."

"Something tells me that with the three of you, I'm not going to be sleeping a lot."

"Cat naps, Kitten. You already know us so well." Kerr grins.

O'Dell kneels down and scoops her into his arms, keeping the towel underneath her ass. "I'll bathe you and put you to bed."

Kerr and I exchange a look and shrug. O'Dell loves shower sex, so we'll give him this one.

After O'Dell and Kyra are upstairs and out of earshot, I use the second towel—Kerr also knows me so well—and clean myself up before grabbing my pants and sliding them back into place.

"This is fucking surreal, huh?"

Kerr shrugs. "The other guys said it happened this way for them, too. As soon as they met their woman, they knew. The hard part was convincing her they could live life this way—that it wasn't a one-time thing or a half-ass relationship."

"Whatever it takes." I rub my stomach.

"We're going to have our family," he agrees.

"*Family*. Christ, now that is fucking surreal. Can you imagine little mini versions of us running around this house one day?"

He nods solemnly, staring into the distance. "Yeah, I can, and it's a fucking beautiful sight."

Chuckling, I elbow Kerr in the ribs. "I just hope they aren't obnoxious like you."

"They will be. I'll make sure of it."

ENTES TUERE
PUNIRE IMPIOS

Chapter Seventeen

KYRA

IT HAS BEEN one hell of a week.

Technically, it's been ten days since we met.

My men are insatiable and thank god, so am I. And because we've been off work for the last week, it has been a fucking free-for-all in this house. I don't even have to do anything seductive to warrant sex.

Bend over to pick something up and there's a hard cock pressing against my ass.

Get into the shower and there's a naked man jumping in with me.

Sit on the couch with a blanket over my legs and there's a man snuggling next to me, slipping his hand underneath the cover to play with my clit.

I'm sore, but in the most blissful way possible. I had no idea the ways I could be stretched, bent, filled, and tempted—but apparently the ways are many.

Also, for the last week, I've had a plug in my ass at least fifty percent of the time. For the first two days, I wore the small one and then graduated to the medium one. Last night, O'Dell worked the large one in and I swear to god I didn't think I could walk.

I did, but I'm pretty sure I look funny doing so.

Tonight is the party at The Access Club, and although I don't give a fuck what anybody thinks about me and my relationship with three men, I will admit I'm nervous about meeting their coworkers and their women. My understanding is that these guys served in the military together at one time or another, and they all served under their boss's command. I guess Victor, their old commander, is recruiting two more teams for the northeast region, and they'll be at the club tonight as well.

"What are you doing, Kitten?" Kerr walks into my sparse bedroom with its humongous bed. We're going furniture shopping tomorrow and they've been showing me custom-made headboards online that they want me to consider. Most of them are heavy wood with eye-bolts in them, and I didn't even know these guys were interested in BDSM or restraints.

Not that it's off the table. I don't know if anything is truly off the table with my men.

"I don't know what to wear to the club."

"Well, women span the gauntlet of clothing options at The Access Club, but the three of us will wear a suit and tie."

"Suit and tie? I've seen you guys in button-down shirts and slacks, but I've never seen you actually put on jackets and ties," Everything below the belt tingles at the idea of seeing my beautiful men all hard and honed with the occasional scar and tattoo classed up in double-breasted suit jackets.

"Yeah, it's pretty much customary at the club. So much so, putting on a tie has a Pavlovian effect on us." Kerr grabs his dick to emphasize his point.

"Oh? I thought I was the one with the Pavlovian effect on you."

His grin widens. "Oh, you do, Kitten. You do."

He stalks towards me, and I put my hand up. "No. Absolutely not. I've already showered and fixed my hair, and I am not starting all over again."

Kerr drops to his knees in front of me, pulling on the ties of my robe and peeling open the sides. "Just a taste."

I suck in my breath and let him push my hips back to the countertop, lifting my left leg onto the padded stool that sits at my makeup counter.

Sweet Jesus, I can't tell them no.

I wonder if I'll ever be able to deny them?

He pushes back my labia and pops out my clit, licking and sucking on the little bud that has been perpetually aroused for the last ten days. "I love worshiping your pussy, Kitten."

"And she loves you worshiping her." I toss my head back, giving myself over to his talented tongue.

O'Dell walks in behind him, takes one look at Kerr on his knees in front of me, and shakes his head. "You're going to make us late, dickhead."

Kerr flashes him his middle finger and continues to tongue and suck on my clit. I breathe heavily and grip the edge of the counter. My newest tactic is doing everything

I can to not let them know I'm close to coming, because I know if they know, they will stop.

But my men are smart and they always know when I'm close.

Kerr leans back on his heels and wipes his face clean. "Fucking delicious."

I don't even complain anymore when they stop, knowing that bitching will only make them drag the torture out longer.

O'Dell smiles at me. "You look beautiful, Cupcake."

I close my robe and blush. These guys can talk about painting my body in their cum and it doesn't bother me, but a genuine compliment and I'm blushing like a schoolgirl. "Thank you, but I don't know what to wear."

"Actually, that's what I came in here for," he offers me his hand, beckoning me to him.

Of course, I give him my hand. I will never not come to or for him when he asks. We walk into the bedroom where a dress is laid out on the bed.

"What is this?" I pick up the shimmery metallic lightweight material.

"Dem and I picked it out while we were out earlier today. Do you like it?"

I hold up the floor-length dress with slits on the sides that go almost to my hips. The neckline is cut low and the blue-green material is shiny and stretchy. Not teal, but literally blue in one direction and green in the other, like an iridescent paint job on a high-end sports car.

"It doesn't leave a lot to the imagination." I frown.

"It's perfect for the club. Sexy, but not too inviting," O'Dell says.

Kerr agrees. "Yeah, because we don't want to kill someone on our first night."

"Do you think a man would actually approach me?" I raise my brow.

Kerr shrugs. "If we gave you room, a man or a woman may approach, but the possibility of not having at least one of our hands on you throughout the evening is highly unlikely."

"Plus, the high slits give us all the access we want." O'Dell grins and now I know their real motivation.

"I presume there will be women wearing practically nothing?"

Both of my men nod. "Yes."

"What about Epi and Leti? What will they be wearing?"

They shrug. "Honestly, we haven't met them yet. This will be our first introduction as well."

"You guys are super territorial with your women, aren't you?"

"Has that not been made abundantly obvious yet?" O'Dell raises his brow.

I giggle. "No, it has, but with you guys, I like it."

Dem walks in fully dressed. His jacket and tie with cufflinks and tie bar are giving him an air of sophistication that makes me weak in the knees.

"Goddammit! Get the fuck out of here and let her get dressed." Then he seems to notice they untied my robe, the sides hanging open. "Has somebody been teasing you, Angel?"

I nod and point at Kerr. I have no problem telling on him.

Kerr smacks his lips with a smile as his response.

"But you haven't come yet, right?"

"No, I haven't come," I whine, but it's mostly for show. I know the game.

"Good girl."

O'Dell reaches around me, his finger going directly to the plug in my ass. Then he taps it a couple of times, as if to prove to himself that it's there. "You're wearing this tonight, yes?"

"Yes, although I hope you'll be removing it later."

"What are you saying?"

"I'm saying, I hope the three of you got us a room, because I want to give myself to you completely tonight, and I want to do it there so I wipe away the memory of any other woman you guys have shared there—because I'm a possessive bitch, too."

O'Dell's green eyes sparkle as he frames my face and kisses my lips. "Cupcake, you erased the memory of every other woman the day we met. And yes, we do have a room. We wouldn't take you there and not give you the full experience. Tonight will be special for all of us."

Dem growls. "Get the fuck out of here and get dressed so we can go."

O'Dell and Kerr chuckle, smacking me on the ass and walking out of my bedroom.

"Do you like the dress, Angel?" Dem looks at me with his gold-green eyes, genuine hope in his smile.

"I've never worn anything like this, but yes, I love it."

"Can I help you get dressed?"

"No, I have to have some surprises for you."

"Okay, Angel. I'll see you downstairs."

AN HOUR LATER, we're inside a private VIP room in the super-posh Access Club with twenty large and lethal men and two beautiful, identical twins who could easily be supermodels.

As a matter of fact, I think one of them kind of is.

"Hi!" The slightly more glamorous of the two walks up and offers me her hand. She's dragging her twin sister behind her, and I can definitely tell who's the extrovert and who's the introvert.

"I'm Epiphany Krushner, but you can call me Epi. This is my twin sister, Leti. You must be Kyra."

"I must be." I shake her hand.

"We can't tell you how excited we are to meet you," Leti says, her voice smaller than her sister's.

"I'm not exactly sure what you've heard."

"Nothing, that's the problem." Epi waves her hand toward the men, half of whom are staring at us. "These men—they either don't know, or they aren't willing to give up the deets. All they told us was we were meeting the other team tonight, and that they were bringing their new girlfriend."

"Yeah, it's a little crazy. Right?"

"We're used to it. But with men like these who have so much to give, it's kind of hard to not want it all the time." Leti blushes, which makes me think about all the sex I've had over the last week, but more so, it makes me think about tonight. I'm so excited, my body is aching to take all three of my men at the same time, claiming them as mine—forever.

Leti's blush also makes me realize that my men's sexual appetites are not unique. The testosterone in this room is so thick, it's almost suffocating and I have to think someone like Leti is feeling overwhelmed by it.

Epi, on the other hand, seems completely impervious to it.

"So, I don't mean to be rude, but you look really familiar," I ask the twins.

"Well, you are seeing double right now." Leti laughs and waves her hand in front of her face. "Sorry, twin humor."

"I'm kind of pseudo-famous." Epi rolls her eyes. "You know, Instagram model, YouTube channel—I have an athletic wear line and a cosmetic line, and I do videos while doing my make-up or trying on clothes. I've been doing it since I was fourteen."

Then it dawns on me. "Krushner Kosmetics and Krushner Kruisers Athletics?"

"Yeah, that's me. Are you a customer?" Epi claps her

hands together. She certainly has the energy of an online social media superstar.

I grimace. "I think I may have tried it at the store, but honestly I can't afford your products."

Epi waves away my embarrassment. "Girl, my shit is so overpriced, even I know it. But you don't have to worry about that anymore. I'll make sure that you get a full kit next week. Although you don't look like you wear a lot of makeup. Your skin is beautiful."

Epi is a tornado of energy, while her sister is the subdued 3D model.

"Um, I don't normally wear much makeup."

"Yeah, if I had your skin, I wouldn't either."

Leti rolls her eyes. "You do have her skin and you don't wear your own product."

"I did tonight."

"But her face serums are to die for." Leti ignores her sister and touches her own face. "Make sure you send her over the skincare line, too."

"You look like you work out. What size do you wear?"

"I..." I've never been good at being given handouts, and although I love my curvy body, I'm a good four sizes larger than either of these women.

Leti seems to get it, reaching out to pat my hand. "We can talk about this later, but we would like to grab lunch with you sometime. As you can imagine, we can't really go out with our old girlfriends and talk about our love lives when dating three men."

I shrug. "I don't have any girlfriends." Although I do

have women from Pemshaw's dojo, I wouldn't call them friends as much as I would call them comrades in arms.

"Well, now you have us," Epi grins as a lean hottie approaches with a tall glass of clear liquid on ice. As if one man moving towards the trio of women requires action, two more men, one of whom is Kerr, walk toward us.

"Drinks, ladies?" he asks, wrapping a protective hand around my waist.

"Come with me, Leti. Victor wants to make an announcement." A soft-spoken man with brown hair, the least lethal looking of the group, nods in my direction politely and then pulls her away, their fingers interlaced.

Kerr kisses my neck. "Lots of testosterone in here, eh?"

"So much."

"Lots of brain damage in this room, too." He chuckles at his joke, but I have to wonder if he's truly joking. They have not given me specifics, but I know they are highly trained to do the nasty things other units don't do. I know if I had wanted Bobby Lash dismembered, it would have happened, no questions asked. Not because they have bloodlust, but because they are so good at it, it wouldn't even phase them to do it. So, if my three men are capable of brutality, then the rest of them certainly are.

"Lots of brain damage, or highly trained and honed power?" I ask.

"Both, Kitten. Both."

The older man pointed out to me as Victor taps his glass to garner attention. "I want to thank everyone for coming. It's been a couple of messy months for our Chicago team and I know you haven't been getting the kind of action you prefer. It seems like we spend more of our time babysitting than rectifying problems the way only we can."

"Seems to be working out for us so far, boss." A big guy pulls Epi into his arms.

"Yeah," Victor frowns. "You guys keep falling in love with our clients and we're going to get a reputation."

I raise my brow, wanting the backstory on that comment.

Dem walks over and offers me sparkling water. "Technically, you weren't our client, so he's not talking about us."

"Anyhow..." Victor slaps his hand on the back of another guy—I'm pretty sure they would both be referred to as a silver fox. "Jacob and I are expanding the business with a slightly different business model in mind. He currently has three teams running out of the Rocky Mountains into the west coast with plans to expand and we're adding another two teams here to cover east, pushing into New York."

O'Dell maneuvers over to us with his brow raised. He whispers, "Head to head with Darian, Xander, and Garrett's business?"

Who the fuck are Darian, Xander, and Garrett?

"No," Victor snaps. "Not head to head. We'll be working with them, collaborating on jobs when necessary."

"Fucking supersonic hearing," O'Dell grumbles while Dem and Kerr laugh.

"Smart ass." Victor shakes his head. "I think everyone's career has overlapped by a year or two, so you should all know each other, if by nothing else than reputation. I'm going to introduce the leads. The rest of you can introduce your teams."

"Lee, Reese, O'Dell, Mateo, Levi—sound off."

O'Dell stands behind me, pulling me into his arms, his chest pressed against my back. Lee introduces Case, Porter, and their fiancée, Epi. Reese introduces Caiden, Soren, and their fiancée, Leti. Then it's O'Dell's turn, and he makes a show of introducing me as his family.

Not girlfriend.

Not fiancée.

Not fuck toy.

Just family.

And no other explanation is required because every man in that room nods their respect.

The final six men, the two new teams, are introduced. I don't know what their stories are, but I can attest that at least two able and willing women are going to be very happy someday.

As Victor wraps up his comments, which include opportunities to move around the country because he intends to set up teams near every major city to work alongside government agencies, the true socializing begins. Quickly, I'm introduced to Epi and Leti's men and carefully, I'm introduced to the new guys. It's at this moment that I see how possessive my men are, but not just my men, all the men. It's fucking weird. Here is a group of men with true respect for each other, who would trust their lives to each other, and yet won't let their gazes linger on a woman that is not theirs for more than two seconds.

It's almost insulting.

I want to jump up and say, *"Hey, I'm more than great tits and a cute ass. You can talk to me!"*

Something tells me that if I did, it would thoroughly piss O'Dell and Dem off—especially in front of these men.

Kerr would probably laugh and then do something super territorial, like bend me over and fuck me right here, snarling at anyone who isn't O'Dell or Dem the entire time.

Yeah, best not to tempt them.

Dem moves behind me, lifting my hair off the back of my neck. He blows cool air against my skin and then kisses me gently. "Are you ready to get out of here?"

"I'm having a good time," I whisper.

"Liar," he chuckles.

"I like Epi and Leti."

He presses his lips against my neck again. "Yeah, they've already scheduled lunch for next week."

"Really?"

"The word is that Epi is pretty pushy and used to getting her way—but she means well."

"Some might say I'm pushy and intent on getting my way," I suck in my breath as he wraps his hand around my waist and grinds his cock against my ass.

"Yeah, that's what we love about you," he growls in my ear.

I've noticed the love word sneaking into our conversations more and more lately. For me, it's perfect. We say it without making a thing out of it.

I love this. I love that. I love you.

And I do. My heart is so full—I had no idea I could wake up this happy every day and fall asleep so sated every night.

O'Dell moves to my side, leaning in to grumble at both of us. "Are we ready to go upstairs?"

"I think everyone is thinking the same thing," Dem says.

O'Dell slyly slides his hand between me and Dem's body, his fingers going directly to the plug in my ass. He taps it again, murmuring in my ear. "Just knowing this is here waiting for me has me so fucking hard right now."

My eyes grow wide, heat flooding my pussy as my gaze darts around the room. If anyone is paying attention, they hide it well. Also, with the way Epi and Leti's men are hovering around them, something tells me they're also itching to get to their own rooms. "Let's get out of here."

Before we can move toward the doors, Victor walks up and offers me his hand with Kerr at his side. "The woman with the beautiful right hook. It's nice to meet you."

"Thanks for not turning me into the Feds for blowing up the house."

He shrugs. "We take care of our own."

I wasn't yours is on the tip of my tongue, but I

already know how my men will react to that comment—similar to how they responded when I said it the first time—so I tamp it down and smile. "Well, thank you anyway."

"I think this party is winding down, but I wanted to introduce myself and say goodnight before I missed you. I hope to see you at future events."

"You will," O'Dell says for me.

Victor nods and turns away.

Kerr leans forward and kisses me hard, pulling me away from Dem and O'Dell into his arms. He's not sly like the others. He's brazen, territorial, and possessive, and I melt into his embrace. Before I can think about it, I'm throwing my arms around his neck, being held up only by his muscular arms.

Kerr flashes me a knowing cock of his brow. "Ready to go?"

"More than ready."

ENTES TUERE
PUNIRE IMPIOS

Chapter Eighteen

DEM

AS SOON AS Victor and Jacob leave the room, it makes it easy for the rest of us to filter out to enjoy our nights. Tonight, we have a room adequately equipped for your basic variety kinkster—an assortment of toys and tools for all your spanking, restraining, and pleasuring needs.

Kyra looks around with her eyebrows up in surprise. "This is nicer than I expected, kind of like a hotel suite."

"What were you expecting?" Kerr closes the door behind us, engaging the lock.

The Access Club staff has a master key to every room in case of emergencies, but they also vet all members and the hall monitors check room guests for ability to consent before allowing them entry, so the locked door is really to let others know they aren't invited. Some people might be into inviting random strangers into their shit, but not us. That's a quick way to get seriously hurt.

"I don't know," she looks up. "Mirrored ceilings, plastic sheets, neon lights?"

I laugh, shrugging off my suit jacket and then loosening my tie. "There's a voyeur room with one-way mirrors and stuff like that. Pretty much anything you're curious about, they have a room to accommodate it."

Kerr, who already has his shirt off, walks up behind her and slides his hands up her arms, pulling at the spaghetti strap ties holding her dress up. "Want to tell us your fantasies, Kitten?"

"I don't know that I have any. My only goal in my sex life has been to come. That's it. Now that you don't let me do that right away, I guess I need to come up with some new ones." She flashes me a teasing smile.

"How about life fantasies?" O'Dell comes out of the bathroom, his jacket off, cufflinks undone.

"What do you mean?"

"Do you want to be married? Kids? Do you want a career, to go to school, own a bar?" I ask, losing concentration as Kerr drops the top of her dress.

"Marriage? Kids? That's a lot to think about right now." She leans her head back onto Kerr's shoulder as he kneads and massages her breasts.

I pull off my shirt and kick off my shoes, approaching her from the front and dropping on one knee, sliding her dress off her hips to pool at her feet. "Whatever you want, we're here to give it to you. Always."

"Right now, I want your wicked mouth on me."

"I can do that, too." I pull her leg up on my shoulder, spreading her thighs so I can bury my face in her pussy.

She smells sweet, like honey, and one swipe of my tongue confirms it. "Honey dust?"

"Mmhmmm," she smiles down at me. "Dessert."

"I have caramel sauce," Kerr slides his knee between her legs and pulls her back against him, spreading her farther for me.

"Later," I grumble from between her thighs, covering her with my mouth and sucking her clit against my teeth. Kyra is beautifully responsive, her moans and hitched breaths one indication of her arousal. Then there is the way her hips involuntarily twitch as her orgasm builds and she instinctively seeks her pleasure.

I slide two fingers inside her hot, wet center, stroking her engorged g-spot until I feel her cunt tightening.

"Not yet, Angel," I pull my mouth away.

She no longer audibly complains, but only grumbles as she takes in a deep, soothing breath. I chuckle as I imagine hearing all the names she's calling me in her head.

"It's time to play, Cupcake." O'Dell, the only one of the three of us completely naked, lifts Kyra out of Kerr's grasp and carries her into the bedroom. I follow behind them, unzipping my pants and dropping them, along with my boxers, to the floor while stroking my cock. O'Dell sits her on the edge of the bed and stands over her. "On your knees, sweets."

Kyra positions herself with her ass in the air for his inspection. O'Dell slides his hand over her beautiful backside, pressing and wiggling the plug, causing her to squirm. "You like that, don't you?"

"I do."

"You like it when we fuck you with it in, don't you?"

"Yes."

"Are you ready to give yourself to us? All of you. Everything you've never given away before?"

Dem and I flank O'Dell as he tempts and teases her, asking questions we already know the answer to.

Kyra looks over her shoulder at us. "Like my heart?"

"I hope to god we have your heart, Kitten," Kerr sits on the bed beside her and kisses her shoulder.

"You do. All of you. So much so that, for the first time in my life, I know I want to be a wife and a mother. Specifically, I want to be your wife and the mother of your children. I didn't think it was possible, but after tonight, I'm realizing that maybe we can have it all."

I crawl on the bed in front of her and pull her into my arms, fucking up anything O'Dell was planning to do from behind her. "I love you, Kyra. You've made me so fucking happy."

"Because I want to marry you?"

"And have our babies," I kiss her with all the emotion rushing through my veins. "I never thought, especially with the lifestyle I'm happily living, that I would meet a woman who wants to have a family. I come from a big Irish-Catholic family, just like O'Dell, but I never thought I'd have one myself."

"Let's be clear," O'Dell interjects, "we are a family regardless of a marriage license or how many children we have. Yes, we want those things, and yes, we are thrilled you want them too, but we are already a family."

I nod my head in concession. "We are family."

"A super sexy family," Kerr leans in and murmurs against her neck.

She shakes her head with tears in her eyes. "We are pretty fucking sexy."

"Yeah, we are," he chuckles and smacks her ass before sliding his fingers down her belly to play with her pussy.

I let go of her so O'Dell can pull her back, her ass bumping up against his hips.

Kyra's eyes meet mine. "Let me taste you, Dem."

Leaning forward, I claim her lips, kissing her breathless and swallowing her gasp as O'Dell pulls the plug out of her. "No teasing tonight, Angel. We're going to take you, immerse ourselves in the moment, and come hard together."

ENTES TUERE
PUNIRE IMPIOS

Chapter Nineteen

O'DELL

I NOD AT KERR, who lies down and coaxes her onto his lap. "Ride my cock, Kitten."

Getting three men inside the same woman takes coordination. We know exactly what works best, especially for her first time. Having Kerr work her from underneath while Dem distracts her with his cock gives me the ability to tease and stretch her to prepare for me. None of us are small men, so she has to be close to out of her mind when I penetrate her for the first time.

Kyra moans as she lowers herself onto Kerr. "Good girl. Now show Dem your talented tongue."

She opens her mouth as Dem threads his fingers in her hair, both men taking it slowly, showing her the utmost gentle care.

I grab the lube off the dresser, dripping a couple drops and then sliding one, two, then three fingers in and out of her. She's worn the training plugs for the last week like a goddess, adjusting to find her pleasure in little to no time at all. The idea of taking her from behind with the plug in always gets me hard, but double penetration is the ultimate gift she can give us. Well, I guess that's not entirely true. Marrying us and having our children is the ultimate gift, but DP requires perfect trust and demonstrates her faith that we're going to take care of her, giving her pleasure while we seek our own.

She moans again, pushing her ass up in offering, riding my fingers while she rides Kerr's cock.

"Fuck, Kitten. You're tightening up on me."

Damn, she's already close. I reach around to find her clit, circling it while pushing the head of my cock against her puckered rosette. "You ready to come for us, Cupcake?"

"I'm waiting for you, O'Dell," she purrs.

"Okay. Relax for me, Kyra. Focus on the pleasure Kerr and Dem want to give you. Push back on me a little." Priming her with the plug all week has trained her to receive me perfectly. She arches her back, pushes out slightly, gripping and sucking my lube-slicked cock inside of her. I slide forward slowly, monitoring her comfort, before shifting my hips and forcing myself balls deep.

She gasps, Dem's cock falling from her lips as she pants, a fine sheen of sweat breaking out on her skin. "Oh, that's so much."

"Shhh. Just relax. We'll wait for you to be ready."

I reach around and circle her clit again until she unclenches, Kerr slowly sliding in and out of her. It takes a minute before she moves her hips, pushing back into me, silently asking for more.

Kerr pulls back to the tip and as he pushes back in, I pull back, the two of us alternating, keeping her constantly full.

"Oh, god," she pants.

"Do you like that?"

"It feels... weird."

Dem cups her face. "Bad weird or good weird?"

She shakes her head. "I can't tell. I'm overrun with sensation..."

I push forward and she groans, letting her head slump forward.

"Do you want us to stop?" I ask, circling her clit faster.

"No!"

Smiling, I give Dem a head nod. He strokes himself, once again lifting her face with a finger under her chin. "You ready to come, Angel?"

"Yes."

"Open your mouth."

Kyra does exactly as she's asked, gripping and stroking Dem with renewed vigor as she wraps her lips around him.

"Mmmm," Dem moans, his eyes closing as she takes him deep.

Kerr and I speed up our strokes, pumping in and out of Kyra faster, her mewls of pleasure vibrating around Dem's cock. Her body clamps down on us as her orgasm hits hard, causing cum to shoot out of my cock, hard and fast. I thrust my hips forward, fully seating myself inside her while Kerr also thrust up with his hips as his cock jerks inside of her.

When he said we've felt everything each other offers a woman, this is what he meant. I can feel his cock pulsing as her body milks him for every drop.

Dem chases his own release, his hands fisted in Kyra's hair as he finally lets go. "Oh, fuck me, Angel. Take every last drop."

She does, because as he often says, she's a good girl.

Kerr and I wait for Dem to finish, releasing our hold on her, when he finally falls back on his heels.

Our woman, our precious angel and precocious kitten, sags onto Kerr's chest, depleted and yet so very full.

She's ours now, fully—the four of us joined as one.

ENTES TUERE
PUNIRE IMPIOS

Chapter Twenty

KERR

AFTER O'DELL PULLS OUT, I wrap my arms around her and stroke her hair. "You okay, Kitten?"

"Mmmhmmm," she murmurs, her dead weight resting comfortably on my body.

"Do you want to take a shower?"

"No. I'm too tired to stand up."

I chuckle. "How about a bath? We'll bathe you and I'll wash your hair."

"That sounds nice."

Dem rolls off the bed. "On it."

With O'Dell and Dem in the bathroom, I whisper in her ear. "Did you like that? Be honest."

"It was intense. I didn't think I could handle it and then I did and came so hard."

"Lots of nerve endings back there—it's a completely different sensation."

Kyra looks up at me, her half-lidded eyes sated. "You'll always take care of me, huh?"

"Always," I kiss her forehead and stroke her cheek, an overwhelming sense of love filling my chest.

"Do you want a big family, too?"

Sighing, I'd like to whole-heartedly agree with my brothers, but I can't lie to her. "I don't know. I had a shitty childhood and part of me would like to break the cycle by giving a kid or twelve an amazing life. But I'm also scared I'll be a shitty father, like the ones I had growing up."

Kyra lifts enough to look me directly in the eye. "You are an amazing man, Kerr. Unbelievably caring with so much love to give, I know you'll be an amazing father, too. But, between you and me, I'm in no hurry to have kids. A couple of little ones would interfere with our naked time."

"There is no rush. Knowing you want them someday will keep the guys happy for a while," I kiss her lips. "We don't want to lose any of our naked time either."

"You ready, Cupcake?" O'Dell walks in wearing a towel around his waist, his hair wet. It's obvious he took a quick shower.

Kyra rolls off me and O'Dell scoops her up in his arms. Carrying her is his second favorite thing to do to her. I think she likes it, too, because it makes her feel small and protected, although I doubt she'd ever admit it. She doesn't have to admit her weaknesses to us; we'll love and protect her no matter what and champion her in what she needs.

"So, this is The Access Club," she says as we sink beneath the soapy water with big frothy bubbles.

I lean against one end of the tub and pull her back against my chest. "Yeah."

"I have to say, I think my bathroom is nicer."

"Are you saying you don't want to come back here?" I wet her hair and massage shampoo through her red locks.

"I mean, I don't mind, but I don't think we need to rent a room to have sex. We have a whole house for that."

She scoots down, leaning the back of her head on my chest as Dem slides in the other end, pulling her feet into his lap and massaging her toes.

O'Dell sits on the edge of the tub, using a soapy washcloth to lather up her chest and slip his hand between her legs. I can tell he's keeping his touch light, because she's not hitching her breath or bucking her hips. She sighs, sinking even further into the water. "It's up to you, Cupcake. Here or home or anywhere else in the world, it's you and us forever."

ENTES TUERE
PUNIRE IMPIOS

O'DELL

"I can't believe we're missing the wedding of the century," Kyra grumbles as we get out of our black SUV.

"Of the century? I think there are maybe twenty-five guests total attending this wedding."

"Yeah, but it's you guys—or guys like you. Three men marrying one woman times two? A double wedding with six grooms and two brides? As Caiden says, that's never happened in the history of ever never."

"Cupcake, you're the one who decided to attend this parole board meeting versus a beachfront destination wedding. We would much rather have you running around in a bikini than facing down this dickhead."

She frowns. "I wish we could have gotten his hearing date moved, but I can't let him or his family think he's getting out. The board needs to see the victim's face."

"We could have taken care of this another way,

Angel." Dem walks up and slides his hand on the small of her back. I shake my head. This conversation is inappropriate, considering the walls we are about to pass through. Victor Townsend's connections can only provide us with so much protection from self-incrimination, but yeah, we could have had Brolin Mann killed a dozen different ways over the last year. But Kyra said no. She wants him to rot in prison for as long as possible.

She wants him to see her face when he's denied parole.

We want him to see our faces, too, because if his parents' money gets him out, he'll be seeing us again.

Kerr is up ahead, holding open the visitor center door to Menard Correctional Center.

It takes a good forty-five minutes to get through security and then be escorted to the parole board meeting, which starts at three. It kills us to do this, but we'll do it for her. Honestly, I'd prefer to never lock eyes with this guy, because I'm pretty sure keeping the three of us in our seats is going to be near impossible. If Brolin so much as looks at Kyra with anything other than absolute fear, I'm sure Kerr will come across the room. Thank god it's being held in a secure facility and we left all our weapons at home. Even something as innocuous as a pen was left behind because we know what we are capable of—given anything rigid or sharp.

Kyra grips my hand as we sit and wait.

"You okay, Cupcake?"

"I'm more nervous than I thought," she whispers back.

"You have your letter?"

She nods. "Yes."

Kyra wrote a letter for the parole board detailing her brutal assault, reminding them of the things Brolin is capable of doing. The DA who handled his case utilized court transcripts to help her craft the right words that will hopefully keep him in prison for the full twenty years.

After that—well, all bets are off.

I'm sitting to her left. Dem is to her right. Both of us are holding one of her hands and not giving a fuck what anyone thinks about it. Kerr sits behind her and plays with her long red hair that's pulled back in a simple, yet elegant braid. He leans forward and rests his forehead against her back.

"Thank you for being here," Kyra says loud enough for all of us to hear. "I know I tried to talk you out of coming, but now that we're here, I'm so thankful to have my husbands standing by."

Oh, yeah—we got married almost three months ago, a week after she found out she was pregnant. She's only now starting to show. None of it was planned, although none of it was exactly a surprise and we just ran with it. On paper, Kyra and Kerr are married, officially making her Kyra Kerrigan, although she never legally changed her last name. Kyra Stewart is our wife and in six months will be the mother of our child and then, from there, who knows?

Three people enter the room and sit at the table while another couple enters through the same doors we walked through. They are wealthy, judging by their clothing, so I assume they are Brolin Mann's parents. Both of them have enough humility to not look Kyra in the eye.

"Parents?" Dem asks.

"Yeah," she nods, her eyes glued to them.

Then a couple of correctional officers walk an inmate in wearing the usual garb. He doesn't look like much, but unfortunately a guy's size doesn't always translate to his strength and it certainly doesn't effectively measure his craziness.

"Jesus. Prison has not been good to him," Kyra mutters under her breath.

"Don't feel sorry for him, Kitten. It's part of the act," Kerr growls behind our heads.

"I don't feel sorry for him."

Dem snarls. "No mercy, Angel."

A court person reads a number of announcements about how this hearing will proceed. The list of convicted charges is read and then Kyra is invited to address the board.

It kills me to let her stand on her own. I exchange a look with Dem and Kerr and know that it is killing them, too.

Kyra stands up, clears her throat, and reads her prepared statement, reminding the parole board and his parents of the heinous and brutal treatment he showed her eight years ago. Hearing the details from her lips fills me with a rage so tenable, bile rises in my throat. I want to kill this motherfucker. I want to take him some-where remote, torture him for fun, and then cut him into small, bite-sized pieces for the local wildlife to feast upon.

Instead, I tap into my calm reserve, take a deep breath, and let it out slowly, hearing both Kerr and Dem do the same.

Then, unfortunately, Brolin gets an opportunity to speak for himself.

Kyra sits between Dem and me, clutching our hands so hard that she damn near crushes my fingers.

Brolin reads from his own piece of paper, his head down. "I'm sorry for what I did to you, Kyra. It was a horrible act committed by a man intent on taking what wasn't his to have. I thought I was in love and therefore entitled to you, but after years of therapy, reading and prayer, I know my actions were nothing more than a product of the privileged life I was born into."

"Are you fucking kidding me?" Kerr growls low in his throat.

I have to agree. I can't believe he's blaming his actions on his wealth and privilege.

Unfuckingbelievable.

"I've spent my time incarcerated trying to better myself by letting go of my anger and resentment, preparing to be a useful tool for society. If I'm released, I will use my education and wealth to help others through the church and by spreading His good word."

Brolin puts the paper down and looks at Kyra and it takes everything within me not to rise up out of my chair. The fucker doesn't take his eyes off her, which only infuriates me more.

"I understand you're married with a child on the way. I wish you all the happiness with your new life. Maybe now you'll let me find my own joy."

Kyra pales, her breathing heavy. "You're a liar and a bully and, yes, an entitled piece of shit, but you deserve no joy. No happiness. No freedom."

"Okay, Mrs. Stewart," Someone from the parole board signals her to stand down. "That's enough."

"He dies," Kerr hisses, and I hope to god there are no microphones in here powerful enough to pick up his threat.

Well, not a threat.

That was a fucking promise.

KERR

We drive home in relative silence, the three of us plotting Brolin Mann's death in our own creative ways. Kyra sits in the back seat with Dem, her own rage simmering below the surface.

Twenty-year sentence, out in eight with weekly check-ins with a parole officer and court ordered sex offender classes. Kyra was granted a permanent protection order—not that she'll need it. He won't last that long and as far as I'm concerned, she doesn't have to know.

He threatened her by letting her know he's aware that she is married with a child on the way. How the fuck could he have known that unless his parents have a private investigator following Kyra, and if they do, how did we miss that?

"Angel, talk to us," Dem says once we're in the house and Kyra makes her way to the stairs.

"There's nothing to talk about," she stops and looks at us, pulling her shirt over her head. "The system sucks, justice is blind, and you're going to kill him, anyway. Don't get caught. I'll never forgive you if he disrupts our family by getting his blood stains on your shoes."

She slides down her pants and faces us in her underwear. "I want to swim. Who's coming with me?"

O'Dell and Dem look at me, but none of us say a word.

I guess that's that. Permission given and received.

"You know I'm swimming," Dem says, unbuttoning his shirt and kicking off his shoes.

"Good, you can make love to me in the pool," Kyra seems to change her mind about going upstairs, shedding her bra and panties at the base of the stairs, and walking straight out the backdoor to our heated pool.

She's diving into the water before Dem can get his pants off.

I glance at my brothers. "What are we going to do?"

"Tonight? We're going to make love to our wife. Tomorrow, we'll have a meeting at work. The less she knows, the better," Dem says matter-of-factly.

"Agreed," O'Dell nods his head and pulls off his shirt.

"I'm waiting!" Kyra calls from the water.

"Goddamn, she's fucking amazing," Dem says.

"She's not okay," I point out.

"No, she's pissed like us, but she trusts us to take care of her like we said we would." O'Dell flashes a predatory grin full of deadly promises. "Fucking perfect for men like us."

Dem, near naked, smacks my arm. "We'll handle this like a family. She's giving us the latitude to do so. Now, I'm going to jump into that pool and make love to my wife. What are you going to do?"

I take in a deep cleansing breath and release it, kicking off my shoes and yanking my shirt over my head as I trip over my pants toward the back door. "I'm racing you there."

DEM

Kyra giving over Brolin's life to us is a gift beyond measure. Because of what he'd done, she was forced to take ultimate control over her life and it's been a struggle for men like us to temper our primal need to beat our chests and take care of our woman.

Don't get me wrong, we still do it, but we're a lot more low-key when we do. The system failed her and now she's handing over the reins to us, her ultimate act of submission.

Couple that with her asking us to make love to her in my favorite spot in the house and yeah, I'm sporting a serious hard on. I'll be angry and vengeful and rage-fueled tomorrow, but tonight, I'm going to make my Angel come so many times she doesn't remember the motherfucker's name.

I dive in and swim the length of the pool, coming up for air as I pull her naked body against mine.

"Took you long enough," she arches her brow.

"Are you cold?" I know she's not; the pool is heated.

"No, just achy."

"Where at, Angel?" I slip my hand between her legs. "Here?"

She wraps her legs around my waist and rides my fingers. "More, please."

I walk over to the edge of the pool and set her ass on the edge of the adjoining hot tub. We've done this dozens of times, so it takes nothing for her to lean back and spread her legs for me. I dive face first into her pussy and lap at her clit, knowing tonight isn't about orgasm control. Tonight, we need to lose control—working out our frustrations through hard fucking and tender lovemaking until all four of us are depleted and fall into a deep sleep.

She slides her fingers into my wet hair, her hips bucking harder with every passing second. "Are you going to come for me, Angel?"

"Are you going to let me come, Demon?"

Demon. That's her little nickname for me after months of me calling her Angel. Honestly, it seems only fitting.

"I want you to flood my mouth and then later soak my cock, sweet girl."

I visibly see her relax, rolling her hips and letting me take her over the edge with a gentle curve of my fingers.

"Oh, yes," she mewls. "So fucking good."

I stand up in the three-foot shallow end, my cock bobbing on the top of the water, and pull her into my arms. She wraps her legs around my waist and sinks down, her heat enveloping my throbbing cock. I claim her lips, sliding my tongue into her mouth, everything about holding and touching her calming the raging beast within me.

"I love you so damn much, Angel."

"I love you, too, Dem."

KYRA

"Do you have room in this pool for two more?" Kerr asks right before he dives into the deep end, swimming the length without taking a breath.

O'Dell walks around the pool deck with a tray of drinks, sitting it down next to the hot tub. He pushes a button and the jets come on, the pool lights changing colors every ten seconds.

Kerr comes up out of the water and kisses my shoulder. I lean back even though I'm impaled on Dem, squeezing and milking his cock with my kegels as he slides in and out of me slowly.

Kerr wraps his arms around me and cups my breasts, stretching me out so Dem can grip my hips and continue to pump into me with smooth, short strokes. They feel so good, instantly melting away the stress and horrors of the day.

I know giving them carte blanche access to take care of the problems in my life is all they've ever wanted, and while I wanted to take care of and protect myself, I can't do it anymore. I'm carrying their child and now there is nothing more important than the life of my unborn baby. My men want to take care of my stresses, the dangers that might lurk in the shadows—well, I'm going to let them.

"Did my Kitten already come once?" Kerr whispers in my ear.

"Mmmhmmm," I purr for him. "Yes, but I need more."

"I'm sure you do."

Dem pulls out and lets Kerr cradle me in his arms, his mouth latching onto my nipple as he carries me out of the pool to the plush cabana swing we have on the edge of the pool deck.

I love this swing. We saw it in a porn shot at a swingers' club and had it custom-built. It's big enough for the four of us, providing a little instability which sometimes turns our sexcapades into fits of laughter. Chuckling as O'Dell fell off the swing mid-thrust into me got Kerr picked up and thrown into the pool. Next thing I knew, we were all swimming—not that it stopped Kerr from instantly plunging his cock deep inside of me.

O'Dell lies down and beckons me to sit on his face, which I now do without hesitation. He licks and sucks until my thighs are shaking around his head; meanwhile, Kerr is kneeling next to me, feeding me his large cock. I lick and swirl my tongue around the head, working him with the same fervor that O'Dell works my clit, the two of us moaning as we approach our next orgasm.

"Give me all that frosting, Cupcake," O'Dell growls as I throw my head back, howling my release to the night sky.

Gasping, I slide down his body and sink down on his cock, Kerr stroking his cock until I'm ready. Leaning forward, I take him as deep as I can, Dem coming up behind me with his fingers slick with cool lube.

"You want this tonight, Angel?"

I nod and moan yes, knowing this is what I need more than anything. I need my men to claim me, mark me, and protect me in every way. I'm theirs and they are mine and together there is nothing we can't tackle and overcome.

He slips his slick fingers inside me, pumping in and out a couple of times before lining up his cock and sliding home. He and O'Dell instantly find a rhythm, alternating their strokes to keep me stretched and full.

"Oh god," I groan around Kerr's cock, but he's not letting me go, threading his fingers through my hair as he fucks my face.

"I love your mouth, Kitten. So fucking amazing."

I look up and try to smile, swallowing down saliva when I can. Dem reaches around me and circles my clit as O'Dell grips my hips, pumping his cock up into me hard. My men know how to move in and out of me beautifully, and it doesn't take long until I'm panting, another orgasm threatening to crest over.

"Yes, come for us, Cupcake," O'Dell growls, his fingers digging into my flesh.

Dem comes with me, shooting deep into my ass as O'Dell pumps into me from underneath, chasing his own release. I cry out in ecstasy, my fist tightening around Kerr, stroking and encouraging him to finish with us. It takes him another thirty seconds as aftershocks tremor through my pussy before Kerr releases his load, his seed hitting the back of my throat. Once he's finished, I let him go and collapse onto O'Dell's chest, panting for breath.

Dem collapses next to us, his hand coming up to stroke my back, while Kerr settles himself on the other side, smiling at me.

"Our beautiful Angel, playful Kitten, and tasty Cupcake—all in one. Love you to the moon and back, Kyra."

"I love you. All of you."

My men, my husbands, the fathers of our child.

Together, there is nothing we can't defeat.

ENTES TUERE
PUNIRE IMPIOS

O'DELL

"Hey brother, this is a nice place."

Ken greets us in the dirt driveway outside the ranch home he shares with Paddy, LeRoux, and their wife, Barbie. Yes, Ken actually married Barbie. "It keeps us busy."

"I'm sure it does."

"So, this is the infamous Kyra." Barbie comes out of the house holding a little blonde girl's hand, followed by LeRoux and Paddy, both of whom we've spent time in the swamps with recently.

Kyra and Kerr exit the SUV with our three and a half-year-old, two-year-old, and newborn. Turns out, our sperm and Kyra's eggs and uterus are a match made in baby-making heaven, but three kids in five years are a lot and we've closed up shop—at least temporarily.

Between having babies, Kyra went back to school and

got a mathematics degree with a minor in education—taking as many online classes as possible while breastfeeding and figuring out her rhythm between working toward her degree and motherhood. Of course, having three husbands helps, and it turns out Kerr has a maternal instinct to rival her own. He really hates it when I say that, but it's true. The boy who grew up with no love, no family, and no nurture has a ton in his heart to give.

"You must be Barbie." Kyra has Maliki wrapped in a sarong against her chest, the four-month-old sleeping soundly despite the long trip.

"Can I peek?" Barbie is a pretty blonde with a certain country vigor that fits ranch life perfectly. Her hair is white blonde, whether it is natural or not, and full of volume even though it's in a braid. Something about her gives me a Dolly Parton glam vibe without the rhinestones or triple-Ds.

Kyra peels back the sarong to show off our sleeping baby.

"Ohhh...." Barbie looks at Paddy, who walks up and shakes my hand in silence, like always.

"We know, we know." He rolls his eyes and shakes his head. Apparently, she's ready for baby number two.

"Hey man." LeRoux, Dem, and Kerr exchange pleasantries while Ken bends down to greet our oldest son, Denton.

"Can we see the horses?" Denton blurts without preamble, hopping up and down while holding on to Dem's hand.

"Right to business, huh?" Ken smiles. "Yeah, let's do that."

The eight of us walk toward the barn with four kids in tow, our little girl, Loralie, wrapping her arms around my legs and demanding to be picked up. The plan is to take the kids horseback riding, let them chase and play with the sheep and goats, and then we'll BBQ with Stiles, Romeo, Bastion, and their wife, Evelyn, who are riding in from Nashville later this afternoon.

My plan is to tire the kids out to the point that we can let them sleep in a tent on the living room floor while we play with our wife in the bedroom. Three kids are a lot and without a family to count on to babysit, finding time to play together has been difficult. Gone are the days of getting naked and jumping into the pool without the thought of who will walk around the corner or when.

We haven't even been to The Access Club in well over a year.

Loralie squeezes my neck when I try to set her down. "Don't you want to meet the goats?"

She shrugs, her shyness taking hold. Their little girl, Emily, who is probably six months younger than Loralie, immediately shows off her pigmy goats wearing matching pajamas. "It's okay. These are really nice."

I stoop down until our daughter feels brave enough to interact with the little girl and her pets. Within minutes, they are best friends and I'm free to focus on the adult conversation around us.

"I was thinking the men could take the kids horseback riding while we relax inside the air conditioning and get to know each other." Barbie smiles.

Kyra looks at me. "Are you guys good?"

"If you're asking if we've got Denton and Loralie handled, then yes."

She saunters up to me, pressing her palm on my chest. "I'll make sure you're good and relaxed later tonight, sugar lips."

Pulling her as close as I can, considering Maliki is resting soundly against her breast, I press a kiss to her neck and whisper in her ear. "Oh, we have plans for you later, Cupcake."

"I can't wait."

After every man takes his turn with his respective woman, Barbie and Kyra walk out of the barn, leaving us with three toddlers.

"Do any of you know how to ride a horse?" Ken arches his brow at the three of us.

I frown. "I'm from the city, but if you can teach a Boston boy like Paddy to ride, you can teach me."

Paddy, who has a thick accent when he drinks—which is really the only time he talks—checks to make sure the kids aren't paying attention and then flips me off.

Kerr and I chuckle. "Let's do this."

Thirty minutes later, they have six horses saddled, three of which they joke are for beginning riders with disabilities.

Fuckers.

LeRoux, who after nearly twenty years away from

the bayou still has a Cajun accent, offers Loralie his hand. "I think it's best if you ride with me, sweetheart."

I nod in agreement. "Smart."

But my daughter only clings to me harder. "I want to be with Daddy."

Ken grabs his daughter by the back of her vest, swinging her up in the saddle before climbing up behind her. She has a helmet strapped to her head.

Paddy hands Dem and me two helmets for Denton and Loralie. "If she insists on riding with you, have her wear a vest."

Protecting Loralie the best we can, I climb up on the saddle and mimic Ken's posture with his daughter while Kerr lifts our daughter into my arms. Then we're off, the six of us riding across a well-groomed trail used for a local equine therapy program.

About twenty minutes in, Kerr grumbles, "How the heck do you keep your balls from being smashed?"

"Well, first of all, you don't sit on them," LeRoux snarks, our son Denton in his lap.

"Now you know why cowboys wear form-fitting Wranglers. It keeps our sh... stuff in place." Ken glances down at his daughter's head and changes his words.

We pass a trio of cabins. Ken waves his hand in their direction. "You guys get the one on the left. Stiles and crew will stay in the one on the right. You can either put the kids in the one in the middle, or leave it empty—"

"Sound buffer," LeRoux breaks in and flashes a knowing smile.

"Looks like Barbie's ready for another one," I throw out.

Paddy's eyes are covered by mirrored aviators, but his lips twitch to give away his thoughts.

Ken nods. "We're working on it, but you know how hard it is to get—" he uses his finger to create air-quotes "—quality time with a toddler in the house."

"Try two toddlers," Dem chirps.

"And yet, you made it work and had a third," LeRoux adds.

"We used to have date nights at the club every month or two, but it's been over a year since the last time we went."

"Let me guess. She won't leave the baby for a night, huh?" LeRoux raises his brow.

"No." I point at Kerr. "He won't."

KERR

Fucking O'Dell.

He's not wrong, but he's still an asshole for diming me out like that.

I shift in the saddle again. Having more babies isn't going to be an option if I don't get off this fucking horse. How do they run fast on one of these things? My nuts are killing me.

I smile at Denton, who rocks in the saddle in front of LeRoux with a huge grin on his face. "Let's go fast, Daddy!"

Oh, fuck me. This is going to hurt.

LeRoux raises his brow. "You trust me?"

I trust him with my life, but the life of my kid is a different conversation. Still, I bet they do this with Emily all the time. "Sure, but I can't keep up."

Paddy comes up between me and Dem. "Your horses will follow ours without much input from either of you. All you have to do is hold on."

I exchange a look with Dem that speaks of my displeasure. "I'm never getting on a horse again after this."

Dem nods. "Agreed."

Ken and O'Dell, with our little girls in their laps, shake their heads. "We'll take the scenic route."

Paddy whispers, "Don't worry, Kerr. We won't be going that fast."

And then LeRoux kicks his horse into gear. Denton shrieks in delight as soon as their horse takes off at a gallop toward the barn. Paddy pursues them and our horses follow suit. I immediately regret climbing into this saddle as I hold on for dear life and try not to let fear screech out of my throat. That would be embarrassing. Put me in full combat gear under heavy fire any day, but not on the back of a seven hundred-pound animal.

The only positive to galloping home is that I'm dismounting the animal faster.

I slump onto the wooden bench, holding my balls.

Dem also dismounts, walking a bit funny himself.

Paddy chuckles as he grabs Denton from LeRoux, putting our son on his feet. "Wimps."

Denton runs over to us. "Daddy, can we get a horse?"

"I don't think they allow horses in Chicago, bud." Dem and I share a look, then look to our brethren, hoping they'll back our ridiculous claim.

"But we saw the police horse downtown," Denton reminds us.

Well, shit. "Uh, those are special."

Kyra and Barbie come into the barn about the same time O'Dell and Ken return. "How was the ride?"

One look at my face and my wife laughs. "Not so much, huh?"

"Never again." I jump up when O'Dell trots in, taking Loralie from him and setting her on her feet. She immediately runs over to the pygmy goats with Emily, her shyness gone. This time, Denton joins them.

"We received a call from Evelyn. They're about fifteen minutes from the house and at the liquor store."

"Campfire stories, tonight? It's been a long time," I say, Dem and O'Dell nodding.

"What are campfire stories?" Kyra raises her brow.

"The times we were deployed together—either on R&R or somewhere else safe—but with lots of liquor and no one listening nearby. We'd inevitably get loose enough to tell outrageous stories. Definitely not safe for kids."

"Not really safe for wives either," Dem points out before kissing Kyra's cheek.

"Sexual exploits?" Kyra lowers her voice so the kids can't overhear her.

"Amongst other things." I slide my hand over her soft, empty belly. She's spent two and a half of the last five years pregnant and I found her pregnancy belly a complete turn on. Of course, she thought I was crazy to lie beside her on the bed watching T.V., my hand rubbing soft circles over her swollen tummy night after night. Thank god she puts up with me.

The roar of motorcycles echoes off the dirt road and barn walls.

"They're here!" Barbie jumps up, clapping her hands together. "You're going to love Evelyn."

Kyra grins up at me as the kids run out of the barn. "It's nice to meet other women in families like ours."

"Yeah, I think you will have a lot in common." I nod.

"Do you know about Evelyn?" she says under her breath.

I don't have to ask her what she means—the look on her face tells me exactly what she's talking about. Nodding slowly, I press my lips to her temple. "I don't know the details, but I know enough to know he is no longer a problem."

"Douchebag problems have a way of disappearing around you guys."

"Funny how that works."

"Hysterical." She smiles and turns with me to follow everyone outside.

We exit the barn at the same time three large men and one petite woman on Harley Davidson motorcycles roll to a stop in front of the house. The little ones have their hands clasped over their ears until the engines are cut off.

Of course, Denton immediately looks up at me and says, "Can we go for a ride, Daddy?"

I don't have the energy to do anything more than shake my head. We have a motorcycle at home and he's been on a few rides around the neighborhood, but he is still way too small to take on a real ride. And I'm definitely not doing it on a dirt road.

All three men wear half-helmets with bandanas over their mouths, while their woman wears a full helmet with a face shield. Evelyn, whom we've never met before—hell, this is only our second time meeting Barbie because we don't mix business and social on the rare occasions we've come down here—jumps off the back of Romeo's bike, pops off her helmet and literally throws it at Bastion, who anticipates her actions, before stooping down to scoop Emily in her arms.

"Auntie Evie!"

"There's my best girl." She blows raspberries onto Emily's neck, making the little girl giggle.

Barbie pulls the woman into her arms and then turns to Kyra, introducing her. Dem and O'Dell are slapping palms with Stiles, Bastion and Romeo and I'm hit with a sense of *déjà vu*.

Well, maybe not *déjà vu*, because I never dreamed all of us would find a special someone who completes our lives and families, yet here we are.

Maybe it's a dreamy sense of nostalgia. Three happy families coming together to create new memories. Teenaged me would never believe my life today.

Bastion cocks an eyebrow and spreads his arms wide. "What? You too good for us?"

"Yes, but I'll hug you, anyway."

Bastion chuckles, murmuring in my ear, "Smart ass."

"Like that is going to change?"

"Who's the little guy?"

"That would be our son, Denton."

"And a little girl?" He motions to Loralie with her light brown hair.

"Our daughter, as well as the baby boy strapped to our wife's chest."

"Damn." His eyes grow big. "Y'all don't waste any time."

I shrug. "All she had to do was remove the implant,

and we had her knocked up within a few weeks. Both O'Dell and Dem are from large families—"

"But Kerr is the one who wants his own soccer team." Kyra walks up and offers Bastion her hand. "Nice to meet you finally."

I don't know what these guys tell their women in regard to some of the stuff we do *on* the clock, but Kyra is well aware of our abilities, considering that two of her problems found their way down here. She doesn't know the details—nor will she ever. That way she can never incriminate herself or us, but she knows enough to know men like us will never stand by idly while working out a problem. And I'm pretty sure she knows who worked side-by-side with Dem and me last summer when Bobby boy struck a deal and got himself put into witness protection.

He served his purpose until he no longer served a purpose.

"The pleasure is all mine. I've heard stories about your right hook." Bastion shakes her hand, his eyes on her face for less than two seconds. That's the thing about men like us. We don't covet what is not ours, and we show respect through a thin veil of indifference. Probably because we all know exactly what kind of men we are. We're cut from the same cloth, no matter what we went through to get here.

"And her left," I add with a proud smile. Kyra and I spar at least twice a week when she's not in her third trimester, and she still visits Pemshaw's dojo at least twice a month, bringing new women in and helping them get settled.

It sucks that it has to exist, but I'm glad that it's there.

"I saw the picture of your black eye. Victor sent it out in the company Christmas newsletter a few years back." Bastion chuckles as Romeo, LeRoux, and Dem walk up, the latter with Loralie on his hip.

"Is he still trying to recruit you?"

"Always." LeRoux rolls his eyes. "I don't know why he wants us on his payroll. We never say no when he calls. It's got to be cheaper to have us on retainer versus full-time employees with pensions and benefits."

O'Dell enters the conversation. "He wants to lock down all the old teams and create a product he can offer to government agencies across the country. But also, I think it's the mother hen in him. He doesn't like not having us under his command, mostly because he worries."

"Colonel Victor Townsend worries about us?" LeRoux arches a brow. That's the thing: these guys aren't in the office with him, so they don't know the ex-military PsySpecOps commander who lost one of his partners, thus disrupting his entire family dynamic. We do, and although Victor rarely shows emotion, there have been times it seeped through his carefully constructed badass exterior.

O'Dell shrugs. "It's harder to protect you from fallout when you're on retainer."

"It's easier to be a ghost when you're not on a payroll," Paddy utters rare, but poignant, words.

Good point.

"Are we ready for food and drink?" Barbie calls out, her voice rising above the din of masculine tones.

Ken walks past her and smacks her ass. "Let's get you guys moved down to the cabins. We're setting up dinner in the middle cabin and using the pit between the properties."

Ten minutes later, there's a caravan rolling toward the east edge of the property. These guys went all out with a pig roast. It takes no time to get our stuff settled, but one look exchanged with O'Dell and Dem, and I snatch Kyra before she can run out the front door to help Barbie and Evelyn in the middle cabin.

DEM

Kerr kicks the door shut after nodding to someone outside. I'm assuming it's Ken or LeRoux, who has our kids with them.

"What are you doing?" Kyra giggles, backing away from me into O'Dell's unmoving chest.

"Having fun?" I purposefully trail my gaze down her body in the lustful way that usually has her melting into me.

"Oh no. We're not doing that right now." Her words say no, but even with Maliki fussing against her chest, she reaches behind her and runs her hand over O'Dell's cock, if the groan he makes is any indication.

"You know," I smile down at our baby—who has my eyes—before locking gazes with her. "Barbie offered to host the kids at their place tonight, to include setting up the crib for Maliki."

Kyra reaches her other hand forward, cupping me through my jeans. "She made a similar offer to me."

"Are we taking her up on it?" Kerr steps forward and cups her face, turning to her so he can claim her lips.

Our ever clever woman strokes me with one hand while kissing Kerr and grinding her ass into O'Dell, all while having our four-month-old who is ready to eat strapped to her chest. Fucking superwoman. "I'd like a night with my husbands."

"We should check with the guys." O'Dell says absently. He's not really paying attention right now as he wraps his big paws around her hips to grind his cock into her ass.

Lucky bastard.

Kerr laughs. "If the tables were reversed, would we have a say in what Kyra tells us we're doing tonight?"

"Good point."

"Now, you guys need to go out there and catch up while I feed Maliki and then make two new best friends." She pushes me back and pulls out of O'Dell's grasp right as Kerr makes a move to slide his hand inside the front of her jeans.

I growl, shifting my erection. "It's times like this that I need a cold pool to dunk in."

She rolls her eyes. "Tell Barbie I'll be over in a few minutes."

"Damn, a whole night with our wife. Won't that be nice?" O'Dell grins, slapping me on the back as we exit the cabin.

"Yeah, if Kerr doesn't fuck it up." I side eye my partner.

"What?" He looks at me like I'm crazy. Don't get me wrong, we all love our children, but Kerr is next level protective of them, which is a lot coming from a guy like me or O'Dell or any of our brethren. We haven't been able to find a nanny that we one hundred percent trust for more than a couple hours at a time. A weekend away, forget about it. And with Maliki being an infant, I'm putting money down right now that Kerr won't last the night before he insists we grab them.

"You know what."

"I trust these men with our lives, so I guess I can trust them with our children."

"Until the morning?" I raise my brow in challenge.

"Bite me, Dem." Kerr walks into the cabin, scooping Loralie into his arms on the way in.

"Come on," O'Dell bumps me on the shoulder. "Let's help get whatever set up."

Three hours later, the kids are tired and cranky and we're out of PG-rated stories to tell. All of our stories revolve around drinking, fighting, fucking, or killing around the world with the occasional prank thrown in. We've told all the pranks we can think of—both the sober and drunk ones—but the kids are old enough to pick up and repeat things.

"How about we go to the house, get baths done and PJs on, and then set up a blanket fort for bedtime?" Barbie and Kyra stand. Denton is sitting on my lap with his head resting against my chest, but I can tell by his breathing he's not asleep. He's listening and cataloging a million questions for later.

Questions, we no doubt, are not going to want to answer.

"You ready for bed, little man?"

"No."

"Are you sure?" I push his hair back and kiss his forehead.

"I'm not tired," Denton protests.

"Well, I am." I press another long kiss to his forehead.

Kerr stands up with Loralie, who is also fighting sleep. "I'll drive you to the house."

Of course he will. Kerr doesn't miss bedtime, not even when we're away on assignment. He always finds a way to video chat, even if it's only for sixty seconds to say *I love you* and *Goodnight*.

O'Dell and I exchange a look of resignation, letting him have this.

"You need help, Cupcake?" O'Dell stands up and takes Loralie from Kerr's lap.

"Grab the kids' bags?"

"Can do."

I help them put the kids in the car and kiss our babies goodnight before punching Kerr lightly in the kidney without saying a word. I don't have to. He knows and doesn't care. Who thought the guy who let his dick lead his young life and was completely shut down emotionally would be the biggest softy of our little family?

Kyra pulls me close. "You and O'Dell should be ready when we get back, or else Kerr and I are going to start without you."

"Kerr is going to start priming you as soon as you climb into the truck." I move her hand to my semi-erect cock. "Besides, I've been ready for hours, Angel. I'm always ready for you."

"One of the many things I love about you."

"We have our phones if you need us." I lean forward and kiss her, closing the passenger door. Kerr takes off, following LeRoux and Barbie back to the house with three kids and one infant. I trust these men with my life, but more importantly, I trust them with my family, which means a thousand times more to all involved.

Paddy, the man of few words, walks up and slaps me on the back. "Let me show you something."

We walk to our cabin. He opens an armoire and then takes a step back. "Candles, lotions, lube, etc."

I shake my head and take a step back. "I think you're great, man, but I'm not interested."

"Fuck you," he grumbles, his Boston brogue coming through now that he's had a couple of drinks. "Barbie threw the basket in here for you, just in case. She knows how hard quality time is when you have kids and she wants you to enjoy yourself. If you want to spruce the place up before Kyra gets back, here you go."

He exits the cabin without paying me a second glance, cursing my name under his breath.

I laugh.

O'Dell walks in, his brow arched. "Why is he calling you a fart knocker?"

I grab a bottle of new, unopened lube and throw it at O'Dell. His eyes grow wide. "Oh. That's weird."

"It's from Barbie, not the guys."

"Well, that makes more sense."

"Do you think Kyra would appreciate some ambience?" I hold up a couple of candles.

"Shit, I know I would. It's been too long since we've gone the extra mile at home," O'Dell says, pulling off his shirt and kicking off his boots. "When's the last time any one of us remembered to grab flowers or something?"

I sigh. He's right. Too fucking right. Kyra has three men and we're falling down on the job collectively. Absolutely no excuses. "Do they need help cleaning up next door?"

He shakes his head. "Nah. They kicked me out. Told us to enjoy our evening, and they'd see us in the morning."

"Ranch life. I bet the guys are close to their bedtimes, too."

"Not Stiles, Bastion, and Romeo. They work nights. So does Evelyn."

I flip a switch and soft twinkling lights come on over the loft bedroom.

O'Dell looks up from his bag, his toiletry kit in hand. "That's pretty."

"Yeah. Maybe we should look at property and build a cabin somewhere. Our own little private retreat where we'd feel safe letting the kids sleep in an adjoining tiny home or something." I look at the ceiling. "I mean, once Maliki is old enough."

"That's not a bad idea. Somewhere within driving distance—"

"Knee deep in the woods with a private pond," I add.

"We can talk about it on the ride home tomorrow." He drops his jeans, but keeps his boxer shorts on. Even though we've been all up in each other's business when it comes to having sex—or in this case, making love to our wife—we don't typically drop trou around each other unless sex is involved. It's just not something we do, especially once we separated from the military and no longer had to put up with communal showers.

"I'll help you set the mood when I'm out of the shower." O'Dell throws me a head nod and then disappears into the bathroom under the loft.

I kick off my boots and pull off my shirt, and then I light the candles, placing them around the bed to include the floor. No kids mean no safety latches. Fire and sharp objects can be at knee level.

Five minutes later, O'Dell comes out of the bathroom with a towel wrapped around his waist and says, "Your turn, man. I'm sure you stink, too."

I roll my eyes and grab my bag, positive I stink. Between the drive, the horses, and the campfire, this city boy definitely feels funky. After brushing my teeth and shaving, I jump in the shower, my mind cycling through the things we could be doing back home to keep the passion in our relationship alive. Kyra's never complained about a lack of effort or attention, and lord knows, we spend every minute we can together. She gets her one-on-one time with Kerr sparring a couple of times a week. O'Dell and I take turns going grocery shopping with her when she wants to go, otherwise we go ourselves. Kyra surprises me in the pool every once in a while, which is always nice. O'Dell likes to take her to the shooting range once or twice a month, but otherwise, we're knee deep in Disney and Pixar movies or other kid activities. Denton is currently in T-ball and starts kindergarten next year. Then it will be Loralie's turn, and next thing we know, all the babies will be in school and/or after-school activities.

Don't get me wrong, I love our life. I love our family. I'm excited about the future. I plan to coach soccer, if anyone wants to play. But how does a family with only one man and one woman do all this and keep their relationship fresh? We have four adults and I'm struggling with how to make Kyra feel special and treasured every day.

"Think you can squeeze me into that tiny shower with you?" Her voice pulls me out of my spiral.

"Hey, Angel. You're back."

"I couldn't wait to get naked with my men." She steps into the shower with me, our bodies pressed perfectly together. Rubbing her thumb over my brow, she frowns. "What's going on in your head, baby?"

"We were talking about how we've been slacking on the romance lately, and it got me thinking."

"About what?"

"How to stop slacking."

She slides her arms around my waist and lays her head against my chest. I grab the soap and lather up my hands, washing her soft skin. "I think we do pretty amazing with three kids. We have a healthy sex life, even if we've had to stop walking around the house naked. We talk every day about the daily grind, but also about our pasts and futures and sometimes really smart stuff like the psychology behind people's motives."

"And sometimes really stupid stuff like politics."

She laughs and brings her head up. "I'm very happy with our life exactly how it is. I don't feel burdened or taken for granted. I feel loved every day, even when you guys are out on assignment. Nightly calls, good morning texts times three. I'm the luckiest woman in the world."

KYRA

Dem kisses my forehead and then my lips before turning me away from him, my back to his chest, but more importantly, my ass to his hardening cock. He runs soapy hands over my chest and down between my legs. "Thank you, Angel. I needed to hear that."

"You're welcome."

His finger circles over my swollen clit. "Did Kerr play with you in the car?"

I chuckle and lean my head back. "Yes."

"Did you come?"

"No. He wouldn't let me."

"Good man." Dem presses a kiss to my neck as he works my clit with pinpoint precision.

It doesn't take long before I'm reaching behind me to wrap my fingers around his cock while riding his fingers. If there was enough room, I'd drop to my knees right now and take him as deep down my throat as possible. Unfortunately, there's barely enough room for the two of us to shower.

"Hurry the fuck up, man," O'Dell growls from outside the door.

I giggle as Dem curses. "Let's go play, Demon."

As soon as we open the bathroom door, O'Dell swings me into his arms and carries me up the stairs to the loft with a king-sized bed and no room for much else. Kerr is stripping off his clothes, yelling, "You better wait for me, fucker."

O'Dell's already laid me down and is trailing a line of kisses over my breasts, latching on to my nipple. "Shower quickly."

Dem chuckles as he climbs the stairs, a towel wrapped loosely around his narrow hips, his hard-on tenting the towel. He immediately sinks to his knees between my splayed legs, putting my feet on his shoulders while using his tongue to draw circles on my inner thigh. "How long can you hold out tonight, Angel?"

"Five minutes?" I murmur, my fingers in O'Dell's hair as he lavishes my nipples with tender bites.

"I'm thinking an hour, at least."

The first flick of his tongue over my pussy has me arching my back. I've tried to explain to him that with three virile men in the house, I'm perpetually aroused and on edge. Technically, I should get credit for time served just by waking up every morning.

Dem did not go for it.

Kerr climbs the stairs dripping wet and completely naked, his cock already hard and jutting out in greeting. He kneels on the mattress next to me, opposite of O'Dell, and smiles down at me. "Hey, Kitten."

I wrap my fingers around him and open my mouth.

"Frisky." He chuckles, his mirth turning into moans of pleasure as soon as I slide my tongue up his length.

Dem does his move that brings me to the edge the

fastest by slipping two fingers inside and stroking my g-spot while sucking my clit against his teeth.

"Ah," I moan around Kerr's cock.

Dem backs off for a couple of seconds, wiping his mouth and looking up at me from between my thighs. "Tell Kerr and O'Dell what you said in the shower, Angel."

"About how I'm the luckiest woman in the world?" I continue to stroke Kerr.

"Yeah."

"I love our life together. You don't have to worry about me, but I promise if I ever am unhappy, I will tell you."

Kerr stops my hand. "Where is this coming from?"

"Dem was worried we were slacking on the romance in our relationship," O'Dell says.

"That's ridiculous. We're the most romantic fuckers there's ever been." Kerr leans down and kisses me, a cocky grin spreading across his handsome face.

Even though we're having a semi-serious conversation, Dem continues to keep me stimulated by rubbing his thumb over my clit.

"And then you said..." He prompts before licking and sucking my engorged bud into his mouth.

I moan, my climax building again as O'Dell moves his hand underneath my ass to circle my hole while biting my nipples. "I'm the luckiest woman in the world."

Kerr's blue eyes sparkling with genuine love. "We're the lucky ones, Kitten. We love you so much. It's indescribable."

"I can describe it," O'Dell murmurs against my breast, his finger using Dem's saliva to lubricate as he pushes past the ring of muscle. "It's all-consuming. The only thing I love as much as you are our children. They give us purpose beyond ourselves."

I'm out of my mind right now, between their ministrations and words of affirmation. "I love you, too. All of you. My life. Everything about it. So. Damn. Much."

Without realizing it, I'm stroking Kerr again, his fingers wrapped over mine. My men have me primed, ready, and although I know Dem would love to drag this out, I really want the power infusion of all four of us coming together. "Now that we've clarified our relationship, can my husbands please fuck me?"

Kerr chuckles. "Perfect precocious kitten, as always."

O'Dell rolls to his back, removing his finger from my ass. "Can you straddle my cock, Cupcake?"

"Do we have lube?" I'm not sure who packed what. We never thought we'd get a night alone to play.

"Courtesy of our hosts." He shows off a tiny bottle and then spreads a couple of drops over the head of his cock.

My eyes flutter closed as Dem pumps his fingers faster, taking me right to the edge before pulling back with a satisfied smirk on his face. "Are you ready to come, Angel?"

"Always."

He helps me sit up and then straddle O'Dell's thighs, who also moved to the edge of the bed, his feet firmly on the ground. O'Dell spreads his legs wide and I straddle him, slowly impaling myself on his rigid cock. After six years of doing this, we've figured out what works and what doesn't, especially with double penetration. I mean, there are only so many ways I can get two of my men inside of me without one of us getting hurt. That's how O'Dell fell off the bed that one time.

I roll my hips, working him in and out of my ass until we're exactly where we want to be, and then he sits up, wrapping his arms around me and pulling me back to lie on his chest. He's not as deep when we are positioned like this, but that's okay, because I'm going to be beyond full in a second.

Dem lifts my legs and places my feet on O'Dell's thighs, spreading me even wider as he pumps up into me. Kerr retakes his position at my head and feeds me his cock, his fingers sliding down my belly to rub my clit at the same time Dem pushes into my pussy. Every movement is slow, and calculated, and sensual, as I feel like I'm being touched everywhere at the same time. Fingers caress my ankles, my thighs, my hips, and my breasts, while my clit gets worked as all three of my husbands pump in and out of me, slow and deep in their assigned hole.

Yes, I said the assigned hole. It's a joke we make sometimes, especially when one of them is missing the action.

My climax builds slowly, but this moment is so much more than a rush to get off—which is what usually happens with three kids to take care of. There is love flowing between us as they care for my body while I, in turn, bask in their pleasure. I wrap my fingers around the base of Kerr's cock and open my eyes, locking gazes with one of the men I love.

He groans. "You feel good, Kitten?"

"So good," I hum, my body relaxed and strung tight at the same time.

O'Dell kisses my shoulder. "What do you want, Cupcake? Fast and hard, or slow and easy."

"More of this." We haven't had the luxury of enjoying each other in so long. I want to prolong this moment. Let us ride this wave of pleasure, our bodies primed, humming with veiled anticipation, for as long as possible.

Dem growls low in his throat. "Fuck, this feels good."

"It's been a long time since we've all been together, taking our time, and not listening for noises outside the bedroom door." Kerr threads his fingers in my hair, rubbing tiny circles with his fingertips against the back of my skull, as if he's tempering his needs like the rest of us.

He isn't wrong. It's been over a year since the four of us could enjoy each other without worrying about who was going to barge in any minute. The Access Club is our haven for that reason, and although I don't need all the other attractions the club has to offer, I do like the ultimate privacy we have amongst the dozens of rooms and hundreds of patrons found within the opulent walls. We really need to find a nanny we trust, but that is hard with four highly suspicious and untrusting people like us.

O'Dell growls against my neck, his thrusts coming a

little faster as his fingers dig into my hips. "You want to come, baby?"

"I can feel you tightening up. I think you want to come."

"I want us all to come, and then I want to fall asleep in a sweaty pile of limbs like we used to."

Dem quickens his pace to keep up with O'Dell, and I stroke Kerr harder, faster, making sure he's with us. When we set our minds to it, release comes quickly, the four of us grunting, growling, and moaning as we get closer to the edge. First, Kerr comes, his load hitting the back of my throat at the same time he tightens his grip in my hair. That pushes me over the edge, my cunt clamping down on Dem, milking him for his seed that he readily gives. O'Dell digs his fingers into my hips, pulling me down as he thrusts his hips up, his cock throbbing inside of me as he shoots his load.

Kerr lets go of me first, immediately laying down beside me and O'Dell and stroking my face. "That's my pretty kitty."

Dem pants, looks around, and grabs the towel he dropped while going down on me. He slides it between him and O'Dell before pulling out, which is really thoughtful considering we're on our friend's bedspread. Otherwise, we'd be leaving behind a huge wet spot. Plus, I'm betting O'Dell appreciates it, considering everything inside of me is going to drip down onto him, anyway.

O'Dell rolls us to our side, sliding out of me as soon as I'm face to face with Kerr. He wraps his arm around my waist, pulling me back into him, while Kerr pulls my knee up, draping my leg over his thigh. I know what comes next. O'Dell will roll on to his back while Kerr enters me slowly, teasing and toying with me until I'm ready for another orgasm. We've done this before, and I'm here for it, but first, I want my men to hear me say it one more time.

"My husbands?"

"Yes, Kitten?"

"Angel?"

"Cupcake?"

I let out a content sigh. "I love you and our life together. Don't ever forget that, okay?"

Three sets of hands touch me on various parts of my body, their touch gentle yet firm. "We love you, now and forever."

PSYSPECOPS
INNOCENTES TUERE
PUNIRE IMPIOS

The Men of PsySpecOps

PsySpecOps soldiers aren't like other soldiers.
They aren't even like other special ops units.
They're a cross of special ops, Intel, EXO, Cyber, and
psychological warfare, to name a few.

Imagine if Chuck Norris, MacGyver, and B.F. Skinner
all jerked off into a test tube and then impregnated
Wonder Woman.
That's would be them.

PsySpecOps doesn't take volunteers. They recruit the
best of the best out of the special forces units.

They are chosen not only for their physical prowess—
marksmanship, hand-to-hand, endurance, strength,
intelligence, instinct, and ingenuity—but also for their
psych profile that says they'll work best as a team.

They're the Army's answer to a super soldier without chemical injections and gamma rays.

Together, the three men psychologically profiled to be a team are a near perfect soldier—accentuating each other's strengths and eliminating any weaknesses.

Rumor has it, ex-PsySpecOps teams prefer to find and share one woman versus date independently. It is said to be an unexpected side-effect of their training.

They functional perfectly as one in all other aspects of their life, so why wouldn't they want to offer the perfect woman a complete package?

The Men of PsySpecOps work hard, play hard, and love hard... all they need is to meet the special woman who can handle all they have to give.

IS THAT YOU?

OUR BRATTY Queen

KAMERON CLAIRE

Our Bratty Queen

I'm the bad twin, the loud one, the one dancing on the tables while my critics condemn me. My family rarely knows where I am, much less what kind of trouble I'm starting, which has left me a lonely shell that I fill with my antics.

My sister is my polar opposite in every way. Quiet and in the shadows, she has everyone convinced she's the good twin, but I know better.

When she is kidnapped, my father hires a security team—three hot guys who don't find my antics cute in slightest—and suddenly, I want to the good twin.

I want THEIR attention.

I want THEIR discipline.

I want to be under THEIR control.

We were hired by a billionaire to secure and protect his twenty-two year old daughter who is the identical twin of a high-profile kidnapping. As it turns out, our charge—the social media influencer herself—was the intended victim. Now, we're a hundred of miles away in a secluded cabin that is off the grid, which means our princess has no access to her phone, the internet, or her legion of social media followers. She's bored, she's bratty, and she's begging to be put over our knees and spanked.

She's also everything our domineering hearts crave—the one woman who speaks to our primal need to tame her into the perfect little submissive. If this security detail only lasted a few hours, we could ignore her antics and control our needs—but as the hours spread into days, and she ups the ante to include endangering herself, we can no longer avoid what is in front of us.

This brat needs to be tamed.

She's ours to punish, ours to tame, ours to claim as our own.

Men of PsySpecOps
OUR WALLFLOWER
Queen
Kameron Claire
USA TODAY BESTSELLING AUTHOR

Our Wallflower Queen

I'm the good twin, the quiet one, the one who hides in the shadows. I never draw attention to myself, never cause my family concern, and most people forget I exist. My sister is my polar opposite in every way. Loud and in the spotlight, she likes to let people believe she's the bad twin, but I know better.

So when I'm mistaken for her, kidnapped and thrust into the spotlight, my three gorgeous rescuers, now bodyguards, are my only protection from the attention I've avoided my entire life—and suddenly, I want to be the bad twin.

I want THEIR attention.

I want THEIR affirmation.

I want THEIR praise.

We were hired to rescue and protect the twenty-two year old kidnapped daughter of a billionaire, but none of us expected to fall in love.

She's everything we've been looking for and more, but we're on the job with a timid and traumatized client, and the number one rule as a bodyguard is *Don't lust after the Client*. Although left unstated, we're pretty sure rule number two is *Don't f^ck the Client*. But the more time we spend together, holed up in a rancher smack dab in suburbia, the harder it is to ignore our feelings, especially as she becomes more dependent upon us, seeking the comfort and physical touch she never received growing up.

She has to know what she's doing to us. She wants our attention, and she's got it. But it's more than that. Our good girl has been lonely her whole life—a quelled bird trapped in a gilded cage with no one to take care of her. We are the men to change that.

And as soon as the threat on her life is dealt with, that's what we aim to do.

She's ours to protect, our to cherish, ours to adore.

KAMERON CLAIRE
USA TODAY BESTSELLING AUTHOR

Our Incognito Queen

She wants her three gorgeous bosses in the dirtiest way. She's forbidden to them, not only because she's their employee, but because she's too pure to be sullied by their darkest desires.

Can one anonymous night sate their needs and fulfill her fantasies?

My bosses are hot, smart, and totally unattainable. But when I glimpse them at The Access Club—New York's hottest underground sex club—and hear a rumor they share their women, I come up with a plan to live out my fantasy, at least for one night.

We have known each other our entire adult life. Bonded since day one of PsySpecOps training, we now own a successful private security business.

We share everything, and we mean, everything. But the one thing we want to share, we can't, because our sweet girl is too pure for the things we want to do to her. We agreed to leave her alone, but when we get a mysterious invitation in the mail, each of us know we're about to get what we want most in this world—her.

One night won't be enough. She's ours to unveil, ours to pleasure, ours to keep.

Sports Romance

Play Action Fake

Quarterback Sneak

Personal Foul

Two-Point Conversion

Red Zone

Man to Man Coverage

The Men of PsySpecOps

Reverse Harem Romance

Our Bratty Queen

Our Wallflower Queen

Our Scrappy Queen

Our Incognito Queen

Our Enduring Queen (pre-order)

Our Indelible Queen (pre-order)

Our Broken Queen (pre-order)

Our Ageless Queen (pre-order)

Hollywood Lights (Pre-Order)

Billionaire Romance

Show Time (Securing Selyne)

Money Shot

Three Shot

Martini Shot

Long Shot

Grayson Enterprises Series

Bedding the Boss

Enticing the Ex

Tempting the Teacher

Wedding the Widow

Short Story Collections and Bundles

Animal Attraction 4-Story Collection

Vegas Nights 4-Story Collection

Last Stand Saloon 4-Story Collection

Instalove Bundle

Fated Mates of SpecOps Sierra

Paranormal Romance

Riding with the Kodiak

Wild Wolf

Cocky Cougar

Broken Bear

Wanted Wolf

Cursed Cougar

Banished Bear

<u>**Fated Mates of Fortune Falls**</u>

Paranormal Romance

The Bear's Wandering Mate

The Bear's Fearless Mate

The Bear's Exquisite Mate

The Bear's Resilient Mate

About the Author

USA Today Bestselling Author Kameron Claire writes stories with witty tongues, wicked needs, and wild deeds. Her paranormal and contemporary books emphasize strong female leads and the protective alpha males who know how to love and support kick-ass, take-charge women. Many of her books contain military veterans, boss babes, dominant men, and goofy K9 hijinks.

Find her everywhere via linktr.ee/kameronclaire
Signed Paperbacks and discounted eBook bundles are available exclusively on her store
Subscribe to the Witty, Wicked & Wild community and read all her books online for as little as $10 a month.

amazon.com/author/kameronclaire

goodreads.com/kameronclaire

bookbub.com/authors/kameron-claire

facebook.com/kameronclaireauthor

instagram.com/kameronclaire

tiktok.com/@kameronclaireauthor